Winter M

A Jaz and Luffy Cozy Mystery

Book 6

Max Parrott

CONTENTS

Chapter 1 1

Chapter 2 15

Chapter 3 29

Chapter 4 43

Chapter 5 56

Chapter 6 74

Chapter 7 89

Chapter 8 128

CHAPTER 1

I t was a tiny, cramped office, with boxes in the corners that still needed unpacking and fine layers of dust left behind by the most recent owner. The walls were thin and let in as much of the chilly winter air as the windows did the festive lights. Even the location was less than ideal—though Blackwood Cove was not a large town, a building on the very edge of it still felt much too far away. There were very few positives that anyone could come up with regarding the cramped space, but to Jasmine, it was perfect.

"I can't believe we have our own office," Jasmine said, shaking her head. "It feels so official."

"Still needs a doggy door," her golden retriever Luffy replied. He couldn't complain much, though—an entire corner of the room had been cleared out to make space for a fluffy dog bed and a food bowl for him. There were even a few toys sprinkled about so he wouldn't get restless. Jasmine had put more thought into his accommodations than her own.

"We'll figure that out," she promised anyway. She had worked extremely hard to open her own office as an official private detective, and she would not cut corners now. "Our first task should be to find some clients, though. We need a good first case to get us on the radar."

"I can talk to some of the dogs around town. They'll know if anyone has problems that need investigating."

"We need them to come to us," Jasmine said, shaking her head. "Remember, we're not chasing down our own cases anymore.

We're going to help people who ask for it, not go searching for trouble."

"Maybe once we find the case, you can convince them to ask for help?" Luffy suggested.

Jasmine shook her head again. Like Luffy, she was excited to get started, but she had read a bunch of books about starting her own business. All of them insisted that if you went begging for your first customers, people would get the idea that your service wasn't good enough to stand on its own. Jasmine and Luffy were already off to a good start with a nice stint of publicity. After all, they did solve Blackwood Cove's very first murder case.

"So, how do you want us to find business?"

"We have to put up advertisements," Jasmine answered, opening a couple of boxes looking for some papers she had misplaced. "I already wrote up a couple of paragraphs about it, and I bet Julie Barnes will give me a discount if I want to put it in the paper."

Julie Barnes was the chief editor of Blackwood Cove's tiny newspaper and had a complicated history with Jasmine involving two separate murder cases. They were on good terms now, and she still owed Jasmine a favor for helping her to relocate. It wouldn't reach a huge readership, but it would hopefully be enough to get her new business off the ground.

Before Jasmine could find the paper she was looking for with her advertisement, there was a knock at the door. Jasmine looked to Luffy and beamed with pride. "Maybe we won't need that advertisement after all."

But alas, when Jasmine opened the door, it wasn't a perspective client waiting to try out their new business. It was only her parents, holding a gift basket with a big ribbon.

"Hey there, Jaz," her dad greeted, carrying the basket past her to set it on her empty desk. "Your mom and I just wanted to drop by and see your new office."

"We're so proud of you," her mom laughed, hugging her. "We always knew you had a bright future, but starting your own business is even more amazing than we expected."

"Thanks, guys. I was at home a few hours ago though... did you really need to come all this way to give me the basket?"

"Your father wanted to see what you've done with the office," her mom explained as her dad walked around in the tiny space.

"Where's this door lead to?" he asked, pushing on a door behind the desk.

"Upstairs. That's where the apartment is."

Apartment was a generous word, as the entire living area comprised the same floor space as the office. Aside from a bed and a tiny bathroom, there wasn't room for much, but the landlord threw it in for free with her rental of the office space. Jasmine was sure her parents would have been fine with her staying at home while she built up the business, but she liked the independence and convenience that the little apartment provided. Besides, it made her feel like a real detective, and she would need that confidence if she wanted her business to succeed.

"I'm going to look around," her dad said, opening the door to a narrow staircase. Jasmine hadn't been able to get the light to work, so as her father went upstairs, he disappeared into the darkness.

"He's just excited for you," her mother assured her. "I am too— I've already started telling everyone about your business."

"Great. The sooner we get our name out there, the sooner we'll be taking on our first case."

"We? It's only you in here, isn't it?"

"Yeah," Jasmine said, with a glance at Luffy. He was just as much a part of the team as she was, but she couldn't exactly explain how she could have full conversations with her dog to help solve cases. "It's just one of those company things, you know? The royal we, or something like that."

"That sounds like one of those things they taught you in those college writing classes. Glad to see they're getting some use."

Their actual use would be in the ad that Jasmine had written. There was a brief lull in the conversation and Jasmine used it as a chance to move around her office, opening a few more boxes in the search for the paper.

"You've certainly brought enough notebooks," her mother said, picking an empty one out of a box Jasmine had left open. "These boxes must have been a pain to get out here."

"I used to work in a bookshop. I managed."

At long last she found the paper she was looking for. The edge was still rough from where she had torn it out of a notebook and the handwriting was messy, but it would only take a few minutes to type up the whole thing and send it to Julie. She might even walk it there herself and step inside for a brief chat. She hadn't talked to Julie in a long while, and she could use some time in a properly climate-controlled building.

"It's not much of an apartment," her father frowned, ducking his head a bit as he came down the stairs. "Quaint, I'd say, or cozy. What are those words that sound sweet but really mean tiny?"

"I know it's small. But the apartment is just where I'll be sleeping. I'll have a lot of work that'll keep me busy, and I know my way around town well enough to find things to do when I'm not."

"Speaking of things to do," her mother said. "Have you heard about that carnival they're bringing to town?"

Jasmine shook her head. She's been too busy getting the paperwork done for the new business to listen to any of the town gossip or even pay much attention to the news.

"Oh, well, it's all very exciting. It's all winter themed and they've got some really nice ice sculptures and fun sled rides for kids. I hear they even have rides and performances and everything that goes along with a usual carnival."

"And it's coming to Blackwood Cove?" Jasmine asked. The town was usually far too small to host anything like that. The only time she could ever remember going to a carnival had been when she was in kindergarten and her parents drove her three hours out of town to spend her birthday at one.

"Your father was surprised by that, too. I told him it was nothing to be too shocked by after all the publicity you and that Marlon Gale fellow brought in."

"They are coming here though," her father confirmed. "In fact, it looks like they'll be setting up pretty close to here. You know that stretch of road between here and the main town area? That's going to be their main area."

"Out where that old field is?" Luffy whined. "That field was one of my favorite parts of this place. Why did we even rent it if I'm not going to have a place to play?"

"Isn't that technically a park?" Jasmine asked, trying to rephrase Luffy's concerns.

"It was at some point, I suppose," her father agreed with a shrug. "But there are really only a few benches around there, and the carnival will only be here for the season. Probably too cold for most kids to be outside, anyway."

"It'll be lovely being so nearby," her mother encouraged, as if she could read the trepidation in Jasmine's voice. "You should look at some pictures online—it's not at all like those traditional carnivals with the bright colors and obnoxious lights—all the ice and snow give it a really nice blue tone; it's almost graceful."

"Alright," Jasmine said. It didn't thrill her, but she knew her parents had no more of a say in the matter than she did. She would get used to the carnival, and then once winter was over, they would be gone and she would be able to renew her focus on her detective work. She imagined that by then she would be a well-established private detective, and she would have far more important concerns than whether a traveling carnival was celebrating next door. Until then, it was good to stay positive about the whole thing. "Maybe I'll even stop by it sometime and see if it's any fun."

"That's the spirit. It can't be much colder than it is in here."

"If it's too chilly for you in here, why don't you and dad head on home? I still need to unpack everything, and I'm thinking of running into town to see if I can get Julie to run an ad in the paper for me."

"We can give you a ride," her father offered.

"It's not far," Jasmine said. "I can walk—maybe I'll even stop in the park and let Luffy get a few final moments of enjoying it before it gets turned into a carnival."

"And you're sure you don't need us to help you unpack?" her mother asked again.

"I am absolutely sure. You guys are acting like I've never been on my own before. I've got this."

"We just want to help you succeed."

"But if we're being stifling, we'll leave you alone," her mother promised. "We'll be at home if you need anything. Feel free to call or just stop by. Heaven knows Lulu would be excited to see you."

"I'll be around often. Just don't make me regret basing the new business in Blackwood Cove."

"Of course, of course," her mother said, finally moving towards the door. "We'll leave you alone now."

"Good luck with this," her father added. "It's a big step, but I know you're ready to make it."

With those final words of encouragement, Jasmine's parents left her alone. She sat down at her desk and leaned back, taking a deep breath. "That was... a lot."

"I think we should go see them next," Luffy said, wagging his tail. "I can play with Lulu and you can talk to your parents more."

"You just want to play with Lulu's fancy new toys."

"That's not true!" Luffy protested, but when Jasmine stared at him, he added: "I also enjoy running around the big house. There's not exactly much space to play here."

"That's what the park was supposed to be for. If you're feeling restless already, we can head out now."

"Yes!" Luffy agreed enthusiastically. "Let's go to the park."

Normally it would have taken Jasmine some time to put on all the jackets and coats she needed to go outside, but it was cold enough in the office that she was still wearing most of the attire. She threw on one extra coat and stuffed the ad she had written into one pocket with her balled up gloves. Once Luffy was done running around in the park, they could head Julie's way and ask about the ad.

Luffy brought his favorite toy along, and when they got to the park, they played a simple game of fetch. It felt remarkably familiar to be standing in Blackwood Cove and playing fetch with Luffy. Though she hadn't known she would return to the town for the long haul, now that she had done so, it felt like the right decision.

She had only thrown the ball a couple of times when she was interrupted by a blond man with a headset and a homely blue sweater. He was both tall and wide, though not astoundingly out of the ordinary in either regard. Jasmine couldn't recall ever seeing him around town before.

"I'm sorry. I don't mean to interrupt, but I'm here to survey the land. I'd prefer if I could do it without the threat of being hit by a tennis ball."

"It's not a tennis ball," Luffy said as he ran up with the ball in question. It was about the right size to be one, but instead of plush it was made of plastic and a smiling alien face printed on one side of it. It was Luffy's favorite toy, and he did not take kindly to the stranger criticizing it.

"I don't think we've met," Jasmine said, sticking out a hand. She was trying not to sound too much like she was accusing him of anything. "I'm Jasmine."

"I'm Peter Rockwell," the man said, shaking her hand. "I'm the owner of Festival Fun, a company specializing in themed carnivals. We're setting up a winter-themed event called *Winter Wonderland* in this park in a couple of days, and I need to get a good look at the land."

"Luffy and I will only be another couple of minutes. He just needs to expel some energy."

"I understand that. Trust me, I would never want to get in between a dog and their owner. However, I need to write up some plans for where everything is going to go, and I've never been good at dodgeball."

"Maybe you could come back in a bit?"

"I'm on a very strict schedule. There's a lot that goes into setting up a carnival in a brand-new location, as I'm sure you could have guessed."

"Yeah," Jasmine said with a sigh. She was getting the feeling she would not win this argument. "How long do you think you'll be around?"

"Only an hour or two. I just need to draw up some plans."

"Hours?" Luffy whined.

"I guess Luffy and I could go run a couple of errands and then come back," Jasmine said. They needed to go see Julie either way, so it would only really be a small disruption of their plans to head there first. "When are you guys setting everything up?"

"Only a couple of days from now. It's all very exciting—I'm sure you'll enjoy the carnival a lot more than this old park."

"I won't," Luffy complained. He put his front paws up on Jasmine's leg to take the ball from her.

"It'll certainly be a change," Jasmine said diplomatically, hoping she came across as being enthusiastic rather than bitter. "I guess I'll leave you to your measurements or your survey or whatever. Wouldn't want you guys to get behind your schedule."

"Thank you. I have to admit, I was worried for a second there that you were going to be unreasonable, but you seem cool. If you're based nearby, please drop by and see the carnival. It's going to be nothing like anything this little town has seen before."

"So I've been told. I'll try to check it out."

She tossed the ball a short distance in front of her for Luffy to chase. Peter flinched as Luffy headed in his general direction, but relaxed again as Jasmine followed suit. She felt a little bad for making him nervous, but after he had kicked them out of the park, she found it hard to be all too sympathetic.

"I don't like him," Luffy muttered.

"I didn't figure you would," Jasmine said as soon as they were out of earshot. "He was pretty nice though, just a little self-centered."

"You can't be both nice and self-centered," Luffy said, pinning the ball under his paws. When he was done talking, he tried to bite through it with his teeth and shook it around a bit. Once satisfied with his victory over the plastic, he returned it to Jasmine and she tossed it out in front of her again.

"It doesn't really matter either way. He said that he runs the company, so he'll probably be way too busy to deal with people outside of his direct circle. That's probably the last we'll ever see of him."

"Good," Luffy said, then grabbed the ball. Jasmine played the modified version of catch with him all the way down to the bookshop and hoped that it would take the edge off leaving the park behind.

The Book Nook was a quaint little shop near the center of town, and Jasmine had a long history with it. From an avid customer to a valued employee to the accidental savior of the shop, Jasmine had been entangled with the Book Nook for as long as she could remember. For that reason, when she walked inside, she was met with a greeting just as warm as the heated air that rushed towards her.

"If it isn't Blackwood Cove's best private detective," Patrick Walker greeted from behind the counter. He was getting old, but the smile on his face seemed to shave the years away. "I'll take it you're here to see Brandon?"

"Julie, actually. Is she around?"

"She should be back in an hour to drop off tomorrow's edition of the paper."

As part of a deal Jasmine had helped set up, Julie Barnes sold her paper at the Book Nook rather than in a building of her own. She had her own section near the front of the shop and the papers were both better organized and better advertised than any of the books that were piled on the shelves.

"Is that Jasmine?" A voice from the jungle of books that made up the shelves called out. Jasmine had to turn to see Brandon, but Luffy recognized his smell in an instant and ran up to him, full of excitement. Brandon chuckled. "I'll take that as a yes."

Brandon looked better than ever. His hair was a bit longer than the last time she had seen him, but it was also more neatly kept. He seemed to have grown into his height, with broader shoulders and arms, though any new muscles were hidden behind a long-sleeved shirt. He seemed happy too, with a glint in his eyes as he lugged a crate of books to the front desk.

"Hey Brandon. How's the business?"

"He's really got a knack for it," Mr. Walker said before Brandon could respond. "He's sending out crates of books every day."

"That's not my fault," Brandon protested. "It's the weather. It's been a pretty nasty spell, and people around here aren't getting any younger. They need some books to keep them busy while they're sitting at home."

"I thought that tourist season was your best season," Jasmine said. When she had been working there, the winter had always threatened to plunge the Book Nook into bankruptcy, and summer had been the only time when the shop had really been viable.

"It used to be," Mr. Walker confirmed. "Brandon here has shaken things up with his new delivery system."

"I offered to lug the books to and from the shop for people and they went absolutely wild," Brandon added. "A lot of the time they don't even have specific books in mind. They just send me in with a genre and ask me to pick something for them."

"It's taken our winter sales through the roof," Mr. Walker said. "Between that and Julie's paper, we've almost got more money than we know what to do with."

"It's only going to get better. Have you heard about that carnival that's coming to town? That's going to drive people into town and out of the house, which are the first steps in getting people through the front door."

Jasmine hadn't considered the exposure that the carnival could bring. If people came from out of town and passed by her office, they might have a case for her. It was certainly more likely than her finding something to investigate in Blackwood Cove, which despite a couple of murders in recent years was still a fairly safe little town. It wasn't enough to get her completely on board, but it lessened the sting a little.

"Do you guys understand why they're coming to Blackwood Cove? We've never had a carnival before."

"Pent up demand, I guess?" Brandon suggested. "I don't know anyone who isn't at least going to stop by and check it out."

"It does look like a wonderful place," Mr. Walker said. "Brandon was showing me pictures on the computer, and I for one am quite glad they're coming here this year."

"Honestly, me too. I love it here, but it's nice to get something new every once in a while."

"Traitors," Luffy pouted.

Jasmine thought about chiming in with her own opinion about the carnival, but the conversation was already moving on.

"You moved into your new office today, right?" Brandon asked, leaning against the counter. "Shouldn't you be unpacking? Or did you already get business and you're here to tell us we're the newest suspects?"

He was joking, but at different times they had both been suspicious figures in cases Jasmine had worked on. She wasn't above investigating her friends if that was where things led.

"I'm actually here to see Julie. I wanted to talk to her about putting an ad in her paper."

"She won't be here for another hour. I'd love to stay and chat that time away, but I've got some deliveries to make."

"Totally fine," Jasmine said. It would have been nice to catch up with Brandon, but she hadn't even counted on seeing him when she dropped by. "I should be in Blackwood Cove for a while, so we should have plenty of time to hang out together."

"And play fetch," Luffy agreed. "Brandon plays the best fetch."

"Maybe we can check out the carnival after work sometime," Brandon suggested, effortlessly lifting the crate of books off the shelf. It was no wonder that Luffy enjoyed playing catch with him —with muscles capable of that, he had no trouble sending a ball flying.

"Maybe," Jasmine said, though the carnival was still not at the top of her priority list. It was getting a little tiresome hearing everybody harp on about it.

Brandon headed out into the cold, and just a few minutes later they saw his car drive by. He still owned the same car since before Jasmine had started college, and it was looking a little worse for the wear. Still, she was sure it would be more than capable of driving a crate or two of used books around a town as small as Blackwood Cove. The shop wouldn't have to make any real investments in his delivery program for quite a long time yet.

"You're free to hang out here while you wait," Mr. Walker offered. "I know it's cold out there this time of year."

"Yeah," Jasmine said, thinking back to her own office and the thin walls. "I think I'll check out the stock. I haven't popped by in a while, so it'll be good to look around."

"Sounds like I might be getting my best customer back," Mr. Walker said with a smile.

Jasmine went to the shelves at the back of the shop and combed through the books. She lost herself in worn out covers and dramatic titles, wondering what she should buy. Meanwhile, Luffy pranced around the shop, sniffing in every nook and cranny to see how things had changed. By the time Julie Barnes showed up, Jasmine had practically compiled her own crate full of books, most of which were old mystery novels. She had never liked them much as a kid or even a teen, but now that she was solving mysteries of her own, she found them a lot more interesting.

"Jasmine Moore," Julie greeted as soon as she came through the door. "I didn't know you were back in town."

"I'm here to stay too," Jasmine said. She hugged Julie through the woman's thick winter coat and quickly explained about her new business. "I was wondering if I could get you to run an ad I wrote in your paper. I don't have a ton of money, but--"

"Are you kidding? We're desperate for advertisers. I'll take your birthday money if you're offering it. Just scrape together whatever you can and I'll have the ad out in the next edition."

Jasmine got out a modest sum. It was more than her birthday money, but it wasn't as much as Julie probably deserved. Julie seemed thrilled with even the relatively meager amount.

"This is great. We needed some new ink."

"I thought your paper was doing better," Jasmine said, worried by the woman's seemingly desperate attempts to get a little more money.

"We are. We shouldn't be going bankrupt anytime soon, but we're still a newspaper. We were never exactly going to be a huge moneymaker."

Jasmine wished she could contest that claim, but even her

writing professors in college had acknowledged that the print industry wasn't going anywhere fast.

"Well, I'm glad I could help at least a little. I still think the paper is pretty cool."

"Me too. And let me tell you, that new carnival has certainly given me a lot to write about. It's the most interesting thing to happen around here in years. I can probably put your ad on the same page as the story on them if you'd like."

Internally, Jasmine groaned. Another convert to the side of the carnival. Had Julie forgotten Jasmine's first ever case and the amazing article she had gotten out of it? That had been more interesting than this weird traveling circus.

She didn't complain though and accepted the offer to be on the same page as graciously as she could. It seemed like the carnival was the hottest trending topic, and she figured she might as well benefit from it.

Jasmine caught up with Julie and Mr. Walker for nearly an hour, and Brandon was back by the time she was heading out the door. He nodded at her as they crossed paths, but said nothing. He seemed pretty focused on his work at the Book Nook, and Jasmine was glad he had found such a good fit.

It had been more than an hour inclusive of all the waiting and chatting, so Jasmine was expecting the park to be free when they returned. Instead, there was a trailer parked in the middle of the park and a half dozen workers in identical blue sweaters roaming around.

"That's not quite what I expected to see," Jasmine said as they got closer.

"We can still play, right?" Luffy asked. "Please? I'll be a very good dog once we're inside."

"I'll talk to them," Jasmine said. She didn't see Peter around anywhere, which was who she would have preferred to talk to. At least he seemed to have been sincere when he said he would be gone before too long. She walked up to a middle-aged man who was carrying a box and interrupted him as politely as she could.

"I thought you guys weren't setting up for a couple more days?"

"Well, the boss came out here to survey the place today, and it turns out there's not much work that needs to be done. This place is pristine. We might even open a couple of days early if there aren't any problems during setup."

"So you're here to stay?" Jasmine asked, trying to hide the disappointment in her voice.

"For the rest of the season," he confirmed, then walked off with his box. Jasmine sighed and walked back to Luffy.

"They aren't going to let us play fetch, are they?"

"It doesn't look that way, buddy," Jasmine confirmed as she led him back to their office. As she sunk into her uncomfortable chair, she sighed. She couldn't wait for the Winter Wonderland Carnival to be over.

CHAPTER 2

Jasmine would not be getting her wish for distance from the carnival. With each day that passed, they inched closer to the opening, and people in town were almost single-minded in their focus on the place. Jasmine's ad seemed to have been completely overlooked, and with so little to do each day, she found herself looking out her window as people stopped by the park to see how the carnival was progressing. As they built up huge piles of snow and walls of ice, it was hard not to find them impressive, but Jasmine held onto her resentment. She was sure that the entry fee would be insane once they were open and commented as often as she could about how they were exploiting the season for profit.

Really, she was just annoyed at their success. She couldn't get a single person in the door, but they had people lining up to see them before they were even open.

On the day the carnival did open, Jasmine was prepared. She had gone down to the library and printed out as many copies as she could of her newest ad and folded them into flyers. She had a thick coat and a bag full of the flyers ready to go an hour before the carnival opened. When people started to line up outside, Jasmine headed out to join them.

Instead of getting in line with everyone who was excited about the carnival, Jasmine walked up and down it. She handed out flyers to the people who were waiting, and since she knew most of them already, she often stayed and chatted. Luffy walked with her, but seemed more interesting in chasing dried leaves as they blew around in the wind than in keeping up with her marketing campaign.

By the time the gates were actually opening, nearly the entire town was there. Jasmine redoubled her efforts frantically to hand out flyers and was beginning to think she hadn't printed enough. She didn't have time to chat anymore, but she did pause for a brief moment when she saw Brandon.

"Hey," she greeted, still holding out a flyer. "Good to see you."

"Oh... Jasmine," Brandon said, clearly surprised. "I thought you didn't want to come to opening day. Didn't I invite you?"

"I'm not going in. I'm handing out these, since everyone in town seems to be here."

Brandon took the flyer and looked it over. He didn't read the whole thing, scanning it for content. "Did your ad in the paper not work?"

"It doesn't look that way. I still haven't really gotten any business."

"That sucks," Brandon said, handing her back the flyer. "I don't know if here is your best bet, though—this Winter Wonderland place is supposed to be all about happiness. I'm not sure anyone wants to think about mysteries they might need help with."

Brandon wasn't the first person to bring that up, but Jasmine figured the sheer number of people she could reach would be more important than their sentiment.

"Maybe they'll read the flyers when they are queuing up for rides later. I'm just trying to get my name out there, so people know I'm here if they need a private investigator."

Brandon glanced back towards the end of the line. He was pretty close to the back, and there weren't many people left that Jasmine hadn't given a flyer to. "You know, this place opens in a couple of minutes. You aren't going to make much more progress in that time. Why don't you come check it out with me?"

"I'm not really interested in the carnival. I would have preferred to have a park for Luffy."

"Come on. You have to admit it looks pretty cool—don't you want to see what they have in there?"

"I'm sure it's all standard carnival stuff."

"Which you have so much experience with that you can just dismiss it like that?"

Jasmine sighed. "I guess not. That doesn't mean I have to check it out though."

"You don't have to. But it will be fun. Come on, do it for me. I didn't have anyone to go with, so if you don't come in with me, I'll have to walk around all on my own. Don't make me do that."

"I don't have the money for a ticket. And they probably won't let Luffy in, anyway."

"No, they're cool with dogs. Didn't you read the flyer?"

Brandon took out a flyer from his bag. Unlike the ones Jasmine had just been handing out, it looked to have been printed at some kind of professional print shop. The paper was glossy and covered in pictures and symbols and folded three ways. Jasmine tried to fight her jealousy as she glanced at her homemade text-only flyers.

"If you check the third panel, they have a whole little section on pets. And don't worry about the admission. It's like two bucks and I can pay for you, no problem."

Jasmine looked at the section of the flyer Brandon was talking about. There was a picture of a dalmatian sitting on a sled with a little girl as an adult pulled them along. Everyone was smiling at the camera and they had put effort into making it look natural and not staged. She had to admit that she was curious about what was going on inside the carnival, if for no other reason than to continue to critique it.

"I guess I could go in for a bit. Just to see what it's all about."

"That's the spirit," Brandon smiled as a cheap speaker recited an announcement.

"Welcome everyone to Winter Wonderland!" a cheery voice said. There was a bit of commotion from the crowd as people started shuffling and moving around. Everyone was focused on the cheap gate in front, which hadn't quite opened yet, separating them from the actual grounds of the carnival. The announcement continued. "We want everyone to have fun, so we're asking all of our guests to follow a few simple rules while you're enjoying everything our Winter Wonderland has to offer."

The speaker rattled off a list of rules, most of which seemed like common sense. As soon as the announcement ended, they opened the gate. It really only led to a ticket counting booth where bracelets were bought and assigned, but it still sent a wave of enthusiasm through the crowd. Jasmine was trying not to share the sentiment, but the excitement was contagious.

"Are you sure you want to go in there?" Luffy asked. "You keep telling me many bad things about it."

Jasmine nodded once. She could survive an hour of the place if it kept Brandon from being lonely while he was there.

As promised, Brandon paid for her admission bracelet, and no one seemed to have a problem with Luffy. The line was moving fast even though people had to buy tickets on their way in, and it wasn't long at all before Jasmine set foot in the Winter Wonderland carnival for the first time.

Her first thought had to do with exactly what she was setting foot onto. It hadn't snowed in Blackwood Cove before the carnival had arrived, but with how the soft ground crunched under her feet, Jasmine was hard-pressed to deny it was exactly what she was walking on.

"They put down a layer of snow in the whole place?" Jasmine asked, looking up to see the rest of the pathways covered in white.

"It's one of their biggest draws. You must not have looked much into this place."

Jasmine wanted to ask a million questions about how they could pull off such a feat and where they got the snow and what they would do if the weather dared to move above freezing. She stopped herself because she knew Brandon wouldn't have any answers, and probably would say it was too cool to matter.

"What do you want to check out first? I know you didn't read the brochure I gave you, but there're all sorts of traditional wintery stuff. They have an entire area completely dedicated to sled racing."

"Sounds expensive. Maybe we should just walk around."

"They had a whole trail made of ice sculptures," Brandon said, the excitement in his voice boiling over. "If you just want to start with some sightseeing, that's where I'd recommend that we go."

"Fine. Come on Luffy, we're going to look at some ice sculptures."

Luffy had just begun frolicking in the snow, but he followed Jasmine obediently after she prompted him to do so. Brandon seemed to know where he was going instinctively, as if he had researched the place before, and he led them across the snowy ground with ease. Jasmine didn't have the right shoes on for snow, and her socks were soaked by the time they made it to the sculpture trail. They marked it with a sign that was meticulously carved out of ice, which felt more gimmicky than impressive.

There was only one entrance, but there weren't many people who had chosen the attraction as their first stop. Jasmine and Brandon were alone as they started down the path, and the only people they could see ahead of them were so far away they may as well not have been there.

"Look at that," Brandon said, pointing to the first sculpture. It was a huge snowflake, about as tall as Jasmine was, with pencil-thin details as it branched out. "You have to agree that it's pretty cool."

"I guess. But nature makes snowflakes, too. Millions of them."

"I guess so," Brandon said, amused. "Maybe some other ones will appeal to you more."

As it turned out, they did. The first part of the path was full of the same icy representations of traditional winter items, but as they moved further down the trail, things got more unique. Someone had carved a campfire out of the ice, and with the way it was lit, it looked absolutely stunning and not unlike actual fire. Past that, there was a whole battle scene. Warriors in medieval armor fought with gleaming swords of ice and thick bulky shields that seemed almost to defy gravity as the puny soldiers held them in the air.

"This is cool," she admitted, staring at how two sculptures intertwined to show one soldier holding a knife to the neck of another. The faces were indistinct, but the effect was undeniably amazing.

"It's awesome. Makes me want to take up ice sculpture. What do you think? Could we sell the products in the Book Nook?"

"You might be able to use them to advertise. Add a giant book under the scene and suddenly you're making a statement about the amazing world that you can find in the pages of a book."

Brandon chuckled. "That's actually super clever. I bet it takes more than a couple of days to get to this level though."

It probably took years, if not decades, and Jasmine wondered how the carnival had managed to get someone that talented to work for them. They didn't seem to be so upscale a place that they would have that kind of money, which made her think those sled races that Brandon had mentioned must have been even more expensive than she thought. She could understand why, if it was contributing towards funding the ice sculpture garden.

They finished the trail, and the exit turned out to be somewhere completely different in the carnival. Jasmine had trouble telling exactly where she was, but they were close to a small Ferris wheel. The center and spokes had been designed to look like a snowflake, and all the cabins were in shades of blue and white.

"We've got to do the Ferris wheel," Brandon declared, already heading in that direction.

"What about Luffy? And don't those things usually cost extra?"

"I'm sure they've got a place where he can wait. And don't worry about the money. I know things are pretty tight for you right now with the new business, and this entire trip was my idea, so I'll cover all the extra charges. Just try to have fun. Who knows when Blackwood Cove will have something fun like this again?"

Jasmine did not want to appear ungrateful if she insisted on not trying out the Ferris wheel when Brandon was offering to pay, so she thanked him and agreed. It had been a while since she had been on a Ferris wheel and it would probably be fun, even if she didn't want to admit to it.

They got to the Ferris wheel, and a bored-looking teenager took payment for the ride. It was only a dollar per person, but Jasmine knew that over the course of all the rides in the carnival, a family could end up spending obscene amounts of money. It was part of how places like Winter Wonderland made their money.

"Is there a place I can leave my dog? He's totally calm, so he can be around people."

"You can tie him to the rail."

"He hasn't got a leash. He doesn't need one."

"He has to be tied up. It's carnival policy."

"Look," Brandon squinted at the teen's nametag. "Rick—her dog is amazing. He will hurt no one. She doesn't have a leash, so maybe you could just keep an eye on him."

"It's carnival policy. Maybe one of you can stay on the ground and watch him."

"I can do that," Jasmine replied. "I don't need to do the Ferris wheel."

"No, that's not fair," Brandon said, turning back to the teen to argue his case. A voice from behind interrupted him.

"Is something wrong?"

Jasmine turned to see Peter, the very first person she had met from the carnival. He was still in his headset and the same blue sweater, which combined to make it look like he was frozen in time. It was surreal, but Jasmine pushed past it.

"It's nothing," she promised. She really didn't want to get dragged into a conversation with him. "My friend is just paying for the Ferris wheel."

"Wait? Are you the same girl and same golden retriever from the park the other day?"

"Yes," Jasmine answered, hoping it wouldn't reflect poorly on them. The last thing she needed was to get Brandon thrown out of the carnival because she hadn't agreed with him easily enough the last time they met.

"I like you guys," Peter said with a smile.

"The feeling isn't mutual," Luffy hollered from the ground. He was doing a remarkable job of concealing his hatred and staying calm, almost as if he knew his behavior was being debated before his eyes. "It's cool that you guys came to check the carnival out. Are you sure there's nothing I can do to make things a little easier?"

"Actually, there is. Could you maybe monitor Luffy for us so we can go on the Ferris wheel? Apparently, he has to be tied up or have someone to watch him while we're on the ride."

Jasmine wouldn't have asked the favor of him, but now that Brandon had done the asking, she watched intently to see what the response would be.

"I actually own the place, so I can't hang around to watch the dog, but I can give him clearance," Peter leaned in to look at his employee. "Hey, Rick. Why don't you let this one wait outside? I've seen him in action, he's a pretty friendly dog."

"Okay," Rick said nonchalantly. He looked at Brandon. "Get in line then."

Since they had been holding up the line to buy tickets, the actual line for the ride was pretty short. They waited only a few minutes before they were let into a bright blue car. Creaking, the Ferris wheel hoisted them into the air.

"I can't remember the last time I went on a Ferris wheel. It has always seemed cool, but I haven't had a ton of chances."

"I think I went on one as a kid," Jasmine said, thinking back to when her parents had taken her to the carnival out of town. She couldn't remember a specific experience with a Ferris wheel, but it seemed like the kind of thing she would have done.

"That surprises me a little. Weren't you a little afraid of heights back then?"

Brandon was correct, and there were still traces of fear left behind. As they were lifted a little higher, she shifted in her seat. She reminded herself that she had faced things a lot worse, but it was hard to avoid listening to the sounds of the machinery. It didn't sound safe, and she had already established that most of their budget was spent on an ice sculpture. What if the place they had recouped that cost was in the construction of the Ferris wheel?

"Ah," Brandon said, glancing at her when she didn't respond as fast as he had expected. "I'll take that as it wasn't only back then."

Jasmine forced a wobbly smile. "I'm good. It's a silly thing to be afraid of."

"You just have to stop thinking about it so much. Try to think about something else. Try looking at the rest of the carnival. It looks pretty cool, right?"

The Ferris wheel was just tall enough for them to see most of the carnival grounds and not much else. The pathways were marked in snowy white, while they had designed most of the buildings to look like little log cabins. A few evergreen trees were scattered about, but Jasmine hadn't been near enough to any of them in person to know whether they were real or fake. It was a very picturesque scene, and for a moment it worked. She was thinking of it like a little model set rather than an actual place far below, and until she realized she did that, she kept her mind off the height.

"I wonder how they managed that. The slides are practically a wall of ice."

Jasmine followed his gaze to a series of ice slides. From a distance, it looked like a super-sized pinewood derby track that had been coated in ice with people in flour sacks rather than toy cars. It was positively huge, and it was inconceivable they could make the entire thing from ice. Jasmine brought that thought up to Brandon and ended up kick-starting a friendly argument about whether they could have frozen something of that size. Jasmine got so absorbed in proving her point she barely even noticed the height anymore. When her feet were safely on the ground again, Jasmine noticed how Brandon was smiling, and realized the distraction was intentional.

"See?" Brandon said as they walked back to Luffy. "I told you it would be fun."

Jasmine couldn't help but agree, at least a little. It had been a while since she had let her hair down, with most of her time going to working on her new business. It felt good to talk and laugh with an old friend.

Luffy was waiting patiently for them, and he bounded up to Jasmine as she got off the ride.

"Did you have fun?" he asked, and Jasmine nodded. Luffy was

wagging his tail an awful lot, and she wondered why. He hadn't been all that excited about the carnival before they had gone on the ride.

"Should we head to the ice slides?" Brandon asked. "That way I can prove to you it's solid ice."

"I think we should check out the food," Luffy said, excited. "I heard someone talking about how there's bacon on all the food they serve here."

Jasmine smiled. Of course, what Luffy was in a good mood about was his stomach. "Heading to the ice slides is a great idea. It'll always be fun to prove you wrong."

They made their way over to the gigantic structure. After their ride on the Ferris wheel, Jasmine was getting a feel for where most things were. The slides were towards the back of the carnival so they wouldn't block anything else off. It wasn't that far of a walk from the Ferris wheel, which was at the center of the park. The snow was being compacted into ice from the constant foot traffic, and Jasmine struggled to maintain her balance on their way there. Luffy handled it surprisingly well, and Brandon didn't have many problems, so she felt rather clumsy as they made their way up to the counter to buy access to the slides.

Instead of an unenthusiastic teen handing out the tickets, there was a man about the age of Jasmine's parents. He was in a wheelchair, but instead of wheels, they had equipped the bottom of the chair with runners like those you would find on a sled. There were ski poles leaning against the counter, which presumably explained how he propelled himself across the snowy pathways of the carnival.

"Two tickets?" he greeted brightly, already counting them out.

"Exactly. We also need to leave a dog out here. We got permission from another employee so we don't have to tie him up."

"Excellent. You're free to leave him wherever you want, but I can keep an eye on him for you if you'd prefer. Sometimes it's good to have a pair of eyes on even the best dogs."

"That would be great," Jasmine agreed. She took Brandon's trick from before and glanced at his nametag. "Thanks, Paul. You're way more chill about this than the last guy we talked to."

"Well, what is the Winter Wonderland about if I'm not being 'chill'?" Paul said, seemingly proud of himself for the joke. Jasmine couldn't help but laugh a little.

"I couldn't agree more. Thanks for keeping an eye on Luffy."

"Honestly, having a dog to keep me company for a while is the opposite of a problem."

Jasmine and Brandon headed towards the slides. The ramp loomed above them, and Jasmine tried to peer through the ice. She couldn't see through to the other side, which felt like it alluded to the whole thing not being made of ice, but it could have resulted from the sheer density of the ice. The stairs they went to were made of steel, and when Jasmine touched the railing, it was stunningly cold. She pulled her hand away. There was enough of a line that they had to stop and wait while they were still on the stairs.

"The bottom looked icy to me," Brandon pointed out. "I don't think there's any way for you to prove this thing isn't completely made up of ice."

They debated more on the topic to pass time rather than to prove a point. When they reached the top and were handed flour sacks to keep their skin from sticking to the ice, Jasmine turned to the woman handing them out.

"Do you know if they made this entire structure of ice?"

"Everything in the carnival is as authentically wintery as it is safe," the woman said cryptically, which wasn't exactly an answer.

"But, like, is this fully ice, or is there some kind of skeleton inside?"

"It's as authentically icy as it is safe," the woman repeated, and the look on her face seemed to convey that she wouldn't be revealing anything else.

"I guess it'll be a mystery forever," Brandon said with a sigh.

Jasmine refused to accept Brandon's premise. She would figure it out at some point, even if that time wasn't now. She had a far more pressing matter of getting into a flour sack and sliding down a slope made of ice.

The rush of chilly wind on her face sent her hat flying off her head as she hurtled down the slope. It was faster than any slide she had ever been on, and it was so thrilling that it tore a laugh from her throat. She glanced at Brandon, and the huge grin on his face said everything about how much fun he was having.

At the bottom, all the lanes of the slide merged into one big rink, and they hurtled across the flat space. There was a snowbank on the other side that caught them, but it didn't give Jasmine much to lean on as she tried to extract herself from the flour sack. Brandon, who had more luck, walked over and helped her to her feet. He held onto her arm as they walked across the ice to the exit, just to make sure she didn't fall.

"That was amazing," she said, shaking her head. She couldn't believe she had ever disliked the place. She was having more fun than she could remember having in ages.

"It was so fun," Brandon said, echoing the sentiment. "I could do it a million times."

Jasmine secretly longed to go for another ride too, but she didn't want to cost Brandon any more than she had to. "Maybe we'll circle back to it later. I was actually thinking we could check out some of their shows. They have those, right?"

"Of course they have shows."

They had made it to Luffy, and the dog walked over to them.

"Hey Luffy," Jasmine greeted, kneeling down to pet him a couple of times. "How was hanging out with Paul?"

"He's fun. He tells a lot of jokes."

"Sounds like you had a good time," Jasmine said, more for Paul's benefit than Luffy's. She knew the man was still in earshot and figured it couldn't hurt to pay him a compliment in return for keeping an eye on Luffy.

"I think there's a cool ice-skating show starting soon," Brandon said, checking the pamphlet he was still carrying around. "We could go see that."

"Sounds great," Jasmine replied. She hoped it would match up to the effort put into the ice sculpting display.

They walked to the rink, which was almost disappointingly small. It was the first time while being in the carnival that Jasmine had really taken in the place's size. With all the bright colors and reflective light, the place felt vast and open while you were standing in it, but she knew it really only took up the size of the park where it had set up base. It was an extensive park, but it still meant the ice rink was small and stadium bleachers were crowding the stands. The metal seats seemed almost to be adding insult to injury, with their frigid temperature stinging Jasmine even through her pants.

"Maybe this was a bad idea," she said after they had been there for only a few minutes.

Unfortunately, it was too late to go back on the idea. The first of the skaters was already coming out onto the ice and leaving would require a huge reshuffling of the crowd, which would be rude both to the audience and the performers. Jasmine resigned to sticking it out and took off her coat to sit on it.

The show itself was pretty good. The skaters were better than anything Jasmine had ever seen, and they had gotten better speakers for this little stadium than for the exterior of the carnival, so the music sounded rich and clear.

A woman dressed in a white and blue sparkling rhinestone outfit was just about to land a jump when someone tapped Jasmine on the shoulder. She had been so engrossed in what she was watching that the sudden interruption startled her, and she missed the perfect landing when she looked to see who it was.

Having expected a family with a kid who needed the bathroom, or someone who just couldn't stand the frigid seats anymore, it rather surprised her to see Peter standing in front of the seat beside her.

"Hi?" she said, as the skater did some kind of very impressive twirl.

"You said your name is Jasmine, right? Is it Jasmine Moore?" Peter asked with no explanation or preamble.

"Yes, that's right."

At this point she had drawn the attention of Brandon, Luffy

and a few strangers who looked rather annoyed with the entire exchange.

"So this is your flyer?" Peter asked, handing over a flyer that Jasmine had handed out earlier.

"Yes, it is. I handed them out to people before they came into the carnival though, so I don't think it can be against any of your rules."

"It's not that," Peter said in a hushed tone. He looked down at the ground, then around at the crowd, then finally back at Jasmine. "We need your help."

CHAPTER 3

After awkwardly extracting themselves from the stands, they stepped off to the side of the path. As the show captivated the audience, they found a quiet spot, and only the occasional person passed by. Jasmine stared at Peter, waiting for some kind of explanation.

"Are you sure your friend needs to be here?" Peter said, looking up at Brandon. "He could go enjoy the show... maybe take the dog with him."

"If you're asking for my help, he stays," Jasmine answered defiantly. "Luffy stays too."

"Um.. right, okay. Here's the thing. We don't want this to get out, because we obviously have a reputation. We sell people a joyous experience, and that's going to be tricky to pull off if people know about the horrible crime that happened here."

"I've heard that before," Jasmine mused. In her experience, people in positions of power were willing to do some pretty awful things to hold on to their reputation. "I am thrilled you want to engage my services, but you still need to report anything serious to the police too."

"We have. And they've agreed to handle this as quietly as they can while still being effective. We're coming to you, because we want this to be over as soon as possible. If you know of any other investigators in the area, we'd love to call them as well. We figure that the more eyes we have on this, the faster we can deal with it."

It was a selfish way of thinking about things, but it was

considerably less awful than some other people Jasmine had encountered. If he had already reported the crime to the proper authorities and wanted to hire her, she didn't see any harm in taking the carnival on as her first case.

"I can work for you," she said with a nod. "Tell me more about this horrible crime."

At the words 'horrible crime', a few people who walked by stopped in their tracks momentarily. They gasped rather loudly at the insinuation and hurried away, keeping their heads low as they muttered to one another.

"Maybe we should talk about this somewhere else. Come with me, I'll take you backstage."

Jasmine glanced at Brandon. He had followed her out of the stands, and she had stood up for him to be there, but the situation didn't have to involve him. If he would prefer to spend his time exploring the carnival, that made perfect sense, and she tried to convey that freedom to him in a single glance. He either didn't get what she was trying to say or would rather stick around, because he followed Peter as he headed into the carnival. Jasmine nodded at Luffy for him to do the same, and they all went as a group towards the back of the carnival. The ice slide was the attraction furthest from the entrance, and Peter led them around the back of it. As he pulled aside a rope for them, they caught the attention of a few of the people waiting in line. Jasmine recognized most of them, which she was sure meant they recognized her. It was just a matter of time that at least some of them could put together her recent ad and her quick trip backstage. She didn't even know what the crime was yet, but she was already doing a pretty awful job of keeping it quiet.

The carnival itself was put together very well, with immersion and theming that felt suited to a much larger theme park. It gave off a sense of establishment and prestige that made it easy to forget it was just a traveling carnival, and when Jasmine was led backstage, she was almost expecting something more. There were a half dozen trailers with doors propped open, a flatbed truck with some patio furniture on it, and a handful of people still in uniform milling about the area. They had tracked the only snow in the area from the main carnival, and it sat in sad, dirty clumps caught in patches of grass. The music from the carnival wasn't pumped into the area, but it was still mostly audible, which left the area feeling vaguely empty and almost haunted. It didn't make her feel better when all the workers stared at them as they passed by.

Peter took them to the furthest of the trailers and knocked on the side of it, since the door was already open. The woman who stuck her head out looked worn out beyond the point of exhaustion. Her blonde hair was pulled up in a tight ponytail, but any illusion of control over it disappeared as it expanded into a wild mess of tangles and frizz. She was clearly in some kind of stage makeup, but it had been smudged and smeared so much it looked more like badly applied face paint.

"Brandy, this is Jasmine," Peter said, gesturing towards all three of them. "She's the private investigator who we found the flyer for."

"Right," Brandy said. She looked poised to break into tears, but she gestured for them to join her in the trailer. "Please, come in."

The steps were steep, and Jasmine's shoes were still wet, so she used the railing to stabilize herself. Luffy put his paws up on the first step after her and waited for her to go further, but as soon as she saw into the trailer, she stopped in her tracks.

There was a dead body in there, propped against the wall like a discarded costume. Sheriff Lustbader, Blackwood Cove's top law enforcement and a fairly close acquaintance of Jasmine's, was standing on the other side of the room, talking to someone else and marking things down in a file. Jasmine turned around and looked at Brandon.

"There's a body in here," she said, not trying to freak him out, but wanting him to know what waited for him if he joined her. Not everyone had seen quite so many dead bodies as her, and she knew they freaked people out even when they were fully prepared.

"The dead man's name was Mark Witz," Peter explained as Jasmine stepped the rest of the way into the trailer. There was not much room, and Jasmine had to be very careful not to run into a small table cluttered with makeup as she moved towards the body. "He worked for us as essentially a stuntman. He was supposed to do things like ice skate down the slides or jump off a building's roof into a conveniently placed snow drift."

"He worked as a stuntman," Brandy verified, her voice trembling a bit. "But he was truly a skater. His grace and talent was always wasted here. I can barely stand the fact he has now lost his life to this place as well."

She was barely holding herself together, and Jasmine glanced at Peter for an explanation of what was going on. Meanwhile, Luffy squeezed past her to get a better look at the body.

"Brandy was married to Mark. She also found the body."

Jasmine's breath caught in her throat. For as many murders as she had played some part in solving, she hadn't really spent much time around the family of the victim. She wasn't very well used to dealing with that particular form of stress.

"I'm so sorry. That's awful."

"Do not apologize. If you must express sympathy, do it by solving the case. I must know who in this depraved camp is responsible for the death of the only man I ever held dear."

Brandy's tone was grave, and Jasmine didn't dare contradict her. Instead, she took a step towards the man's body, already noticing the first sign that something was wrong.

"What's that discoloration around his fingers?" Jasmine asked, kneeling to get a better look at the area of his skin. "It looks almost purple."

"It's frostbite," Sheriff Lustbader answered, walking closer. He seemed to have finished whatever conversation he had been involved in before and was now walking over to talk to Jasmine. "It's a strange sight on someone found indoors."

"They seem to leave the trailer doors open most of the time," Jasmine pointed out. "The cold could easily have gotten in, and he's not wearing much winter gear."

Mark was wearing the same blue sweater as everyone at the carnival, but he had no gloves and his shoes were just as ill-suited for the snow as Jasmine's. Despite that, Jasmine surmised it would have taken a much colder day to turn the lack of preparation into frostbite.

"Frostbite's not a fast process," Lustbader said. "If he forgot to put on gloves, he should have noticed the symptoms and gotten warm long before it got that bad."

"It has to be connected to the cause of death then. Do we have one yet?"

"There's nothing obvious. The company hired a forensic investigator from outside, and I'm trying not to move the body around too much until she gets here."

"It'll be hard to get much further without that information."

"I know. There's a broken window that places this solidly as a suspicious death, but I have gathered little more. I've started a few interviews while I was waiting."

"Broken window? Where?"

Before the sheriff could answer, his eyes went to somewhere behind Jasmine. When she followed his gaze, she saw that Brandon had entered the trailer.

"Brandon?" Lustbader greeted, sounding surprised. "I expected Jasmine to show up eventually, but I have to admit I didn't think I'd see you here."

"I felt weird waiting outside. Can I help?"

Jasmine looked between Brandon and the body, scanning him for any kind of reaction. He seemed to be doing fine.

"It's probably best you go back to the carnival. It's brave of you to want to help, but it's a murder investigation. It's not quite the place to play detective."

If he had worded it any other way, Jasmine might have agreed with him and sent Brandon away. But with his accusation that Brandon was trying to play detective, it reminded Jasmine of countless other times they had accused her of the same thing. A fierce need to defend him welled up within her.

"If he wants to stay and help, he can. Consider him part of my investigative team if it makes you feel better."

"Jasmine..." Lustbader shook his head. His disappointment seemed to condemn her for even letting Brandon come close to this. She understood the impulse, but it was only fair Brandon got to make that decision for himself.

"If you want to help, you can look for anything suspicious. If you want to go, that's alright too."

"I can look around a bit. It can't hurt to have another pair of eyes on the case."

As he spoke, Jasmine noticed that his eyes went to the body. He didn't react physically, but she thought she saw a change to the look in his eyes. It only lasted a moment, and then it was gone, with Brandon turning to get a better look at things.

"I'm going to take a look at the broken window," Jasmine said. "Shout if you need me."

Jasmine scooted her way to the back of the trailer. There were too many people around for it to be a simple process, but once she was near the broken glass, things cleared out a bit. Lustbader had put a few yellow markers on the ground where the glass was spread, and Jasmine was careful to stay a safe distance away. She didn't know what they had photographed, and she didn't want to disturb any potential evidence. Even though Jasmine was now an official private investigator, she was pretty sure there would be trouble if anything she did was considered interfering with the investigation of the actual police.

"Why do you think they would break a window?" Jasmine mused, turning to Luffy to see if he had any ideas. Except, as it turned out, Luffy hadn't followed her across the trailer and was over with Brandon and Lustbader. She figured it would have been hard for him to squeeze past everyone, but it still felt unnatural to not have him by her side.

"Were you talking to me, or am I missing a headset somewhere?"

Jasmine turned around and saw the girl that Lustbader had been talking to a moment before. She was a young teenager, maybe thirteen or fourteen, judging by the way she looked. Her blonde hair stuck out from under a knit hat, and she was wearing a pretty thick winter coat. Her eyes were strikingly blue, standing out even at a distance.

"Uh... neither, I was just talking to myself," Jasmine said, though she filed away the idea of getting a headset. It would allow her to talk to Luffy in public without casting too much suspicion. "Who are you, exactly?"

"I'm Diana," the girl said, sticking out a hand. "My dad kind of owns the place, so I hang around here instead of going to school."

At the mention of her father, Diana pointed towards Peter. Jasmine could see the resemblance, though Diana wore the same features with far more grace.

"By here, do you mean the active crime scene?" Jasmine asked, wondering if Diana had seen the body already.

"I don't normally frequent here, but I guess I am today. As for the window, I think they needed to get a weapon in and out. They could just walk in the open door, but someone might still notice a weapon."

"There are no signs of injury from any kind of weapon on the body."

"Maybe they were really precise. How close have you looked?"

"Close enough to tell whether he was stabbed," Jasmine answered. Though she was dismissing it, Diana's weaponry idea wasn't bad. Maybe it hadn't been a knife, but there were a lot of things that someone wouldn't want to draw attention to directly before a murder. They had also broken the window from the outside in, which would make sense if someone was trying to toss in a tool to use later. The only reason she wasn't giving the theory more credibility was to keep Diana from poking around the crime scene. Brandon was different, he was an adult, not a curious teenager. "You should probably go back to whatever you normally do. We can handle this."

"I know. It's just so *boring* out there. I want to do something interesting for once!"

"There are lots of interesting things you can do that don't involve death,. Why don't you go find one?"

Diana hung her head and stomped out of the trailer. Her dramatic exit might have been more effective if she did not have to weave through the people blocking the way. Jasmine turned her attention back to the broken window, and the glass scattered on the floor. There were no noticeable patterns, and it didn't look as though the glass had been kicked out of the way, or trailed through the trailer in a significant way. Carefully, she took a step forward to get a closer look at the window frame, where the glass had once been set. There was a scrape along the bottom, a pretty deep scratch considering it was gouged into hard plastic. It started from the left, close to the center, and she followed the path it made down to the ground. The glass seemed just a little more concentrated there, which made sense. But something else caught her eye. She kneeled down to get a closer look, and her suspicions only grew.

There, just in line with the scratch, was one shard of glass which had not broken off as cleanly as the others. It had more of a tapered edge and was thinner than the harsh shards on the ground. Jasmine leaned closer and gently set a finger against the out-of-place shard, confirming her expectations—it was ice, not glass.

The carnival was full of ice, but there wasn't much of it backstage. It was certainly something to go on, so she wrote it down. She could figure out later exactly what it meant.

At that precise moment, a shriek from Brandy interrupted Jasmine.

"Get that thing off my husband! Get it away!"

Jasmine's head snapped towards the body, instantly curious as to what Brandy had seen. She was just in time to see the woman grab Luffy by the collar and pull him back away from Mark's body. Jasmine hurried over, hoping to right the situation.

"What's going on?" she asked, hoping someone would give her a clear explanation.

"That dog you let in was sniffing around the body like it was some kind of treat," Brandy said, practically hauling Luffy by the collar to get him away from her husband.

"I was just looking for clues!" Luffy defended as he caught his breath again.

"I'm sorry," Jasmine said, turning to Brandy. "I should have warned you, Luffy is part of my team. He sniffs out anything suspicious and helps me know where to look for clues. He wasn't trying to disrespect your husband, he was only trying to help."

"Is he officially trained for this, or is there as much chance he'll pee on the body as finding anything important? I was polite for not yelling when you brought him in, but you're forgetting that my husband was a person. He deserves respect."

"Of course he does, ma'am. It's just that Luffy--"

"Jasmine, could I talk to you outside for a moment?" Lustbader interrupted. He didn't sound angry, or like Jasmine was in trouble, but his tone was stern enough that she immediately agreed. They stepped out of the trailer, leaving Brandon and all the carnival workers inside.

"Luffy was really trying to help. She really shouldn't have thrown him like that."

"I know. You're a good kid, and Luffy's an obedient dog, but you have to remember that Brandy just lost her husband. She's trying to grieve, and any invasion on that is going to sting. If she wants Luffy to sit this one out, he needs to wait on the sidelines for a little while."

"He's part of my team."

"I know, and I would say the same thing if you had a human partner who was upsetting her. When she goes home or back to work or wherever she needs to go to work through this, you can let Luffy sniff around all you want. Until then, you need to respect what she's been through."

Jasmine stared at the ground. It didn't exactly seem fair to Luffy or to her that he wouldn't be able to help, and she wanted to protest that it could solve the case much more quickly. She knew that even if it was true, Lustbader still had a point. Brandy was grieving and as irrational as that could be sometimes, she had a right to handle it in whatever way she needed to.

"I understand. Maybe Luffy can investigate a bit out there."

"You're banishing me outside?" Luffy protested, putting his paws up on her leg. "You can't do that."

"That sounds like a great idea. I'm going back inside. You can come back in once you get things all sorted out with Luffy. It would be very polite of you to apologize to Mark's widow when you come back."

The way he phrased it stopped it from sounding like a command, but it was clear from his tone he expected Jasmine to make an apology before she continued with the investigation.

Lustbader stepped back into the trailer and Jasmine looked down at Luffy, ready to make a different apology.

"I know I need to stay out here so I don't upset the widow."

"That's true. But it's also more than that. It looks like the back window was broken from the outside. If you can go back there and sniff around the area back there, you'd be doing me a huge favor."

"Really?" Luffy asked, wagging his tail at the prospect of being helpful.

"Really. I need to stay here and look around the scene some more, but we need to check that area too. You can get a head start on that."

"I can do that. I won't let you down."

He started off around the trailer to begin his search, and Jasmine stepped back inside. Brandy was being consoled by Peter, and Jasmine walked up to them. They both stopped talking to stare at her.

"I just wanted to say that I was sorry about Luffy. You shouldn't have to see anything like that while you're still mourning your husband."

"Thank you," Brandy said, wiping her eyes. "I hope I didn't hurt him. I just... I couldn't stand seeing him there, treating my husband like a piece of meat."

Jasmine wanted to defend Luffy, but she stopped herself. "I understand. You don't have to justify your feelings."

"You're a sweet girl. I'm so glad you're on the case."

Jasmine thanked her for the compliment and excused herself to get back to the investigation. Brandon was standing against the wall, looking vaguely in the body's direction, but he didn't seem to investigate all too closely.

"Have you figured anything out?" Jasmine asked, directing the question both at Lustbader and Brandon.

"I've been marking things down for the paperwork," Lustbader answered. "Trying to make a plan for solving this."

"That's smart," Jasmine turned to Brandon. "What about you? How are you doing?"

"Do you think it's weird that he's sitting up? I always imagined that dead bodies would lay horizontally."

In Jasmine's experience, dead bodies were usually in that orientation, but she didn't see it as a point of interest. People died in many unique positions, and it didn't always align with how they were killed. She didn't want to discourage Brandon from doing his best, so she nodded.

"It is unusual. I'll mark it down."

She got her notebook out of her bag. There were still some flyers loose, and one of them dislodged as she tried to get out her notebook. It fluttered to the ground, but a draft from the open door pushed it towards the body. Gently, it landed right next to Marks' hand, close enough to be within the area of investigation. Jasmine remembered how much it had upset Brandy to think Luffy was disrespecting the scene. She knew her advertisement sitting so close to the body could have the same effect, so she hurried to remedy the situation. As she got closer to the body than before, she accidentally shifted the arm ever so slightly outwards. The wrist now faced Jasmine directly, and there was a bit of space between the sleeve of the sweater and the body. It was in that space she noticed something strange. Gently, she turned his body a little further and pulled back the very edge of his sleeve. It was hard to see because there was no sign of blood or a scab, but there was a gash in the man's wrist, following the line that connected his hand to his arm. It wasn't too deep, but it should have bled.

"What are you looking at?" Brandon asked, stepping up.

"There's a weird cut on his wrist. But I don't see any blood on his clothes or in the wound."

"It must not be recent then. Maybe it's not related to his death?"

"No, it's more than a scar. It looks like a cut into his skin."

Brandon stepped forward, and Jasmine held his sleeve back so

Brandon could see what she was talking about. He frowned when he saw the perfectly bloodless cut.

"That's weird."

Jasmine missed having Luffy around. She turned to Lustbader to see if he had anything to add. He looked down for the first time, and his eyes widened when he saw Jasmine's hand on Mark's sleeve.

"If you're going to be moving the body, you should really be wearing gloves. It would also probably be a good idea to leave it in place until the forensic investigator they hired gets here."

"Okay. I'll keep that in mind, but in the meantime, can you come look at this? He's got a fairly deep cut, but there's no blood around."

Lustbader sighed and walked over, still holding his file folder out as if he was ready to go back to writing notes at any point. His brow furrowed at the sight of the wounds.

"That's odd. If you're not seeing any trace of blood, there's a good chance that he didn't die here."

"Yeah," Jasmine agreed, letting go of his sleeve. "Another reason to place it as a suspicious death."

"Exactly. There's a lot of work to be done."

The sheriff walked back to his corner and to fill out more paperwork. Jasmine had hoped he would have given a little more input, but he seemed more consumed by procedure than speculating about what could have happened. Jasmine needed either a new perspective or some additional information. As Brandon and Lustbader weren't helping her with the former, she went to Peter to see if she could get the latter.

"Would Mark normally have been in this trailer?" she asked, glad that Peter had separated himself from Brandy and was now available for questioning. "Or was this reserved for other people?"

"All of our performers came and went from this trailer freely. It's where many of them put on their costumes and make-up. Mark wasn't in here more often than any of them, so it's definitely not surprising to find him here."

"If all of your performers come through here, it must be pretty busy. Is that right?"

"I would imagine so. I don't spend all that much time here, but I would think it gets quite crowded during the morning hours."

"Just the morning hours?"

"Well, perhaps before each show too, but this isn't a place where people hang out. It's strictly functional—there's not enough room for it to be anything else."

"So if something suspicious was going to happen in here, it would have to be between shows," Jasmine said, thinking out loud.

"I guess so. I know that Brandy found the body when she was coming to give her makeup one last once over, before going out on stage."

"When was that?"

"Just before that show that you went to. She was the only skater who didn't do the morning show, so she was the only one who came back to the trailer. It's really awful that she had to be the one to find her own husband's body."

"Brandon and I went to the eleven o'clock show. So if Brandy was here before that, the body was here before ten-thirty. When was the morning show you were talking about?"

"Nine-thirty. Some people only come for the shows, and we wanted to make sure they had something to do as soon as the carnival opened."

"So the skaters probably would have been here around nine to get ready," Jasmine said with a nod. "That only leaves about an hour and a half for the killer to have left the body, maybe even an hour."

"Left the body? Don't you mean to kill?"

Jasmine knew what she meant, because it didn't seem plausible someone had killed Mark during that timeframe. With such a tight window, it would have been hard to commit the actual murder and take care of any cleanup. Combined with the bloodless gash on his wrist, it looked like this was the scene where the body had been dumped, not the scene of the murder.

Before Jasmine could explain herself, there was the sound of footsteps coming up the stairs of the trailer. Jasmine thought it might be Luffy, returning prematurely from his mission, or perhaps Brandy deciding that staying at the scene was too much to bear. In the doorway, however, was neither of them. Instead, there was someone else entirely, a tall woman in a lab coat, with a big medical bag looped around her arm. She wasn't smiling, and she looked around the doorway of the trailer as if she was as much a stranger to it as Jasmine. It didn't take long for Jasmine to realize who she was.

The forensic scientist had finally arrived.

CHAPTER 4

L uffy was quite proud to have been assigned such an important job. He had investigated on his own before, but usually it was because Jasmine couldn't be there. This time, she had chosen him for the job, even though she could have tagged along. He was aware it was mostly banishment from the trailer, but that didn't negate the importance of his job.

The back of the trailer was very close to the edge of the park. They were far enough away from the center of Blackwood Cove for another road to act as the absolute end line of the area. The plant life grew thicker back here, turning the open field of the park into more of the droopy forestry that filled the spaces between towns. The trees were scraggly, but there was also plenty of underbrush and even some thorns that made the whole place unwelcoming. Luffy had to be careful as he walked around behind the trailer, making sure he didn't hurt his paws by stepping on some of the rougher underbrush. It was not particularly overgrown behind the trailer, but Luffy needed to keep his eyes peeled as there were enough stray vines which were attempting an escape from the forest.

He found the window without too much trouble, though it was too far up the wall for him to see inside the trailer. Instead, he focused his eyes on the ground nearby, sniffing at the grass for any sign that someone else had been there. There was nothing unusual, but when he got closer to the window, he noticed an indentation in the dirt. It wasn't a full footprint, and with the grass in the way it was hard to tell whether it was anything at all. Someone had been standing there, but Luffy had found nothing yet to explain who they were or why they had been there. He would need to keep looking if he was going to find something good for Jasmine.

Standing near the footprints, Luffy put his paws up on the side of the trailer. He had been hoping to get a better view of the window, but he found something much more interesting. There was a scuff on the side of the trailer, a rubber mark that tennis shoes left on a basketball court if a player changed directions too fast. Luffy was not particularly well versed in sports, but he could tell that someone's foot had pushed against the side of the trailer at some point. There was no way to tell whether it had been recent or was from an event long past, but Luffy committed it to memory. Satisfied, he put his paws back down on the ground.

At that moment the wind changed, and Luffy got a whiff of an entirely fresh scent. It seemed to come from under the trailer, and he ducked his head to get closer to it. He could barely squeeze underneath it, and it wasn't a comfortable fit even when he did. The smell was stronger now, and it reminded him of the crimes he had helped Jasmine solve in the past. It smelled like blood, but it didn't seem to come from anywhere in particular. Instead, it almost emanated from all around him. The ground beneath the trailer was flaked with ice, but there didn't seem to be anything else under the caravan. It drove Luffy crazy as he couldn't figure out exactly what he was smelling—he was sure it was blood, but it was too faint for him to place. Even if it had been buried, he should have been able to tell where it was coming from.

While he was under the trailer, he noticed an extra pair of feet walking towards the trailer. He didn't recognize the shoes as belonging to anyone he had seen inside, or even anyone he had seen in the carnival. He watched her step up onto the stairs and wished he could be in there with Jasmine to relieve his curiosity. Turning back to the task at hand, Luffy determined that he would have to do an even better job of the task Jasmine had assigned to him. If she saw how good he was at searching for clues, she wouldn't banish him outside the next time.

He was about to go back to look at the window, but just before he turned away, someone left the trailer. This time the pair of feet were familiar—they belonged to Brandy, the widow. Luffy was sure of it, and he was pretty sure she was the only reason he wasn't allowed inside. Since she was leaving, he could probably head inside. He needed to wait for her to get away far enough so she wouldn't see him go back into the trailer. As he watched her walk a few paces away, hopeful that soon he would be allowed back inside, she turned around and came back. She repeated the move a few times, then adjusted her path, so she was pacing horizontally back and forth in front of the trailer. Luffy's spirits dropped. He would never join Jasmine inside if Brandy stayed right in front of the door.

"Hi, Danny," Brandy blurted. Luffy jumped, and he looked around for the newcomer. There was no one in sight, human or animal, to whom she could have been addressing. Absurdly, she continued. "Yes, I'm here."

Luffy realized after only a moment more that she had to be on the phone with whoever this Danny was. That would be the only reason she would have to justify her location to someone.

"It's awful, Danny, it really is," Brandy said, and Luffy felt bad for listening in on her grieving. He prepared to head back to the window, but before he could, she continued. "I just feel so guilty."

Luffy didn't know everything about humans or their emotions, but he knew guilt stemmed from doing something wrong. If Brandy was feeling guilty about the death of her husband, that might mean she had something to do with it. He crouched down to listen more.

"You're right," Brandy said with a sigh. "Thank you so much, Danny. I needed to hear that."

A long pause ensued, then she continued: "That would be great. I'll head that way now. You're a lifesaver."

Brandy walked away from the trailer, and this time she didn't turn around. Luffy took this as his opportunity to come out and hop back up the steps. No one seemed to notice him as he sauntered in, so he walked over to where the body was. He recognized the shoes of the stranger from before, a woman in a lab coat who was kneeling next to the body. She was holding up Mark's wrist and looking at the same cuts Jasmine had pointed out.

"That's odd. Usually you don't see this unless someone was trying to stage a suicide."

"You've seen something like this before?" Jasmine asked. "I'd never seen a cut like that with no blood."

"That is pretty odd, but it could result from the blood being drained. I was talking about placing of the cuts. It's not deadly, but a lot of amateurs think it will be. Some killers will place cuts there to make it look like a suicide."

"Which this isn't. There's a broken window, and no blood. It can't be self-inflicted."

"Right. Which is why this is baffling. If they wanted to not arouse suspicion, they wouldn't have set things up to look like this."

After a few more seconds of examining the cut Jasmine had found and the identical one on the opposite wrist, the woman moved on to check the body for other bits of evidence. She put a few gloved fingers to Mark's throat, as if checking for a pulse that they all knew wasn't there. After a few seconds, she tilted her head.

"Interesting."

"What is?" Jasmine asked, pencil poised above the page, ready to write something down.

"His body temperature feels colder than it should," the scientist replied. She took off one glove and reached a hand into her bag, pulling out a scanning thermometer. When she aimed it at the chest of the body, the screen flashed blue. She shook her hand as she read off the number.

"His surface temperature is reading three degrees colder than the air temperature. That's really unusual."

"What should it be?"

"It varies, usually based on how long the person has been dead for, but it's almost never colder than the outside temperature. The body would have to have been stored somewhere with significantly colder temperatures than what we're seeing, and probably for a long time. Since it's already pretty cold, it also wouldn't surprise me if there were some ice crystals in his chest when we open him up for the autopsy."

"Is that how he died? Did they freeze him to death?"

"I don't think so. Look at this."

She pointed out some discoloration around Mark's neck. Jasmine squinted as she stared at it. "Is that more frostbite? Like on the fingers?"

"I don't think so. I think it's bruising which has resulted from strangling. There's a lot going on here, so I'm not going to call it the official cause of death until I have more information. But if you're looking for a fast answer to help with your investigation, that's what I would assume based on what I'm seeing."

"Thank you. I don't want to get in your way, so I might go get started with some interviews. Could you email me a copy of your final report?"

"Yeah, of course," the woman answered, and there was a brief exchange of information. Jasmine tucked it away in her pocket and headed towards the door. That was when she noticed Luffy had come back inside.

"Hey, buddy. I didn't realize you were in here."

She continued out of the trailer, and Luffy followed. They managed a few paces away before she started talking.

"I thought you were investigating the broken window. What were you doing back inside?"

"I saw Brandy leave. I thought it would be okay for me to come back."

"Maybe. She could have come back, and I would have looked like a terrible person for letting you back near her husband when I knew she didn't want that."

"Actually, about Brandy--"

"Hey, Jasmine, wait up!"

They looked back to see Brandon, hurrying in their direction.

He caught up with them pretty quickly, but the effort left him out of breath.

"I wasn't really sure what to do in there. You were the one to bring me with you, so I thought maybe it would be best if we stuck together."

"Oh," Jasmine said, sounding a bit surprised. "I was going to do some interviews. I guess there's no reason you can't come with me."

"Cool. I'm excited to see more of your process."

"I think we should go talk to Brandy," Luffy said. "I know we saw her earlier, but I heard her talking on the phone and she said she was feeling kind of guilty. I think--"

Jasmine shot him a look that seemed to implore him to keep quiet. They had company, and it was a tall order to balance talking to the both of them. Luffy wasn't thrilled that Brandon took priority, and it didn't help to hear how their conversation went.

"Who are you going to start with?"

"I want to talk to the skaters who were preforming in the morning show. They were in the trailer before the body was dropped off. They might have noticed something out of the ordinary, or they might just be able to give us a hint about what the ordinary looked like for them while they were there. That would help us pick out any inconsistencies between how things are supposed to be and how they are now."

"That's a great idea," Brandon agreed, and from there they chatted about things Luffy couldn't care less about. He was still peeved that Jasmine hadn't even asked him once what he had found over by the broken window. When he had heard about the blood, possibly drained out of the body, it had made him think about the smell of blood under the trailer. He wanted to talk to Jasmine about her potential theories, but she was too busy chatting with Brandon. They discussed what kind of figure skaters the place used and whether any of them were poised to find success anywhere other than the carnival. Luffy hung his head and walked with them silently.

The area with the trailers they had just left behind was the only stage area for the carnival, but the ice rink was also off limits to anyone who wasn't an employee. This, of course, did not apply to Jasmine, and she walked up to the edge with her notebook. The women who had starred in the show were skating around the arena, picking up props they had left on the sidelines and setting things back up for their next show. Jasmine had a tricky time getting anyone's attention, but she eventually caught the eye of a short woman with auburn hair that had been pulled back into a bun. She skated over to Jasmine and leaned against the railing.

"Hiya. We're not supposed to talk to people between the shows, because we have a lot to do."

"I'm actually a private investigator. The man who owns the carnival hired me and gave me permission to talk to whoever I needed to."

"Oh... okay. Do you want me to get one of the others for you? Annette and Henrietta probably know more about pretty much everything. Eve and I are just junior performers."

"That's alright. I just wanted to talk to you a little about the trailer where you normally get ready."

"The trailer where I normally get ready, or the trailer where the older skaters normally get ready?"

"Older?"

"Annette and Henrietta. They're professional skaters, so they get ready in the main trailer. Eve and I usually just get ready with Diana since she had her own room in her dad's trailer."

"Are you not a professional skater?"

"I'm as good as one, but I'm only thirteen, so they can't call me one."

With the makeup and the reality that figure skaters were often pretty small, some of her childish features had been easy to dismiss, but looking at her now it was hard to make the same mistake.

"But you still perform? Isn't that against some kind of child labor law?"

"Since we don't stick to one state, that's always changing," the girl said with a shrug. "Most of the time, since I don't get paid and

I'm on property anyway, I can get away with it."

"I can't decide if that's crazy cool or really messed up," Brandon said, shaking his head.

"It's crazy cool."

Another girl skated up behind her. She was an inch or two shorter, but sported the same shade of auburn hair.

"This is Eve, my little sister. And in case I forgot to mention, I'm Charlie."

"Eve performs too?" Jasmine asked, wide-eyed. The girl looked tiny. "How old is she?"

"She's eleven. If there are ever any throws or lifts, she's the one that goes in the air. They used to hire guys as skaters, but they haven't needed to ever since I was old enough to be thrown."

"That's crazy," Brandon shook his head.

"It's really fun," Eve said, and when she smiled it became clear she was growing one of her adult teeth. It was a stark reminder of exactly how young she still was. "What are you guys talking about?"

"This lady's a private investigator," Charlie said, pointing at Jasmine. "I don't know who the guy is, but he kind of seems like he's with her."

"What are you guys investigating?" Eve asked.

"Just something that happened in the trailer where the skaters get ready. Do you think you could get me one of them?"

"Yeah, sure," Eve said and skated off. Charlie stayed where she was.

"So," she said, tilting her head. "Can you tell us any more about the case? You don't have to worry about Eve, she's really grown up. She can handle this sort of thing."

"Well--" Brandon started, but Jasmine cut him off.

"I'm sorry, but it could compromise our investigation if we told the wrong person the wrong thing. It has nothing to do with your age and everything to do with making sure we solve the case."

"Is that true?" Luffy asked from where he was still moping at Jasmine's feet. He had never heard her reference any rule like that before, and the two girls seemed pretty young to be getting information on a murder investigation. Sadly, as it seemed to be a theme while Brandon was around, she ignored Luffy.

"I got someone," Eve declared, skating forward with a new face that clearly belonged to someone much older. She wasn't particularly tall, and the variation between her height and Charlie's was not huge, but it was clear they had finally gotten through to an adult.

"I'm Jasmine Moore. I work for a local private detective company, and I wanted to talk to you a little about--"

"Ah, yes, I know exactly what you're going to ask about. Is it okay if I send the kids to go finish packing up?"

"But Aunt Annette, we want to hear about the mystery too!" Eve whined.

"You sound like a baby when you do that," Charlie said in an accusatory tone, trying to mince her words as an insult. "They're never going to let you look at anything if you fuss about everything."

"You can send them off to do whatever they need to," Jasmine agreed.

"Girls, go finish getting ready for the next show. Make sure Diana is ready too. She needs to go on for Brandy," Annette said, shooing them away.

"Why is Diana skating again today? Didn't she do the morning show?" Charlie asked.

"She just is. I've already talked to her father about it, so don't worry. Just get everything ready."

When they were gone, she looked to Jasmine. "I'm assuming you're here about Mark."

"You already know about him?"

"Of course I do. His wife was supposed to perform with us during the last show, but Peter came to us five minutes before to tell us she couldn't make it. There wasn't even time to get Diana suited up to take her place."

"Diana, as in Peter's daughter Diana? I think I've met her. Does she perform too?"

"I know it seems weird," Annette said, already on the defensive.

"But the kids really love skating, and they're good in front of an audience. They're still getting their education and everything, they just do school in the evenings."

"I'm not here to talk about that."

"You might want to check up on the legality of it before you talk to the real cops, though," Brandon recommended. "They'll be coming through to ask their own questions."

"Our lawyers can handle that one. For now, what do you guys need to know about Mark? I was pretty close to the guy, so I can tell you a lot about his schedule."

"That's great," Jasmine said. "For right now though, we want to talk about your schedule. You were in the usual trailer to get dressed and put on your makeup before the show this morning, right?"

"Of course. We all try to go there before the shows so we can help each other with the entire process. It can be a lot to replicate every morning."

"Did you see anything unusual this morning? Were any of the costumes out of place, or something mysteriously knocked off a table?"

"No. It's a pretty tight fit in there, so we all keep a pretty close eye on what we do with our stuff."

"If you walked through the place, do you think you'd be able to point out anything that wasn't where it was supposed to be?"

"Yeah, for sure. I can't come with you now though, we've got less than an hour until the next show. If I take off the skates now, I won't have time to get back and warmed up again."

"There's a man dead," Brandon shot back in a tone that sounded a tad bit too harsh. "Don't you think that's more important than--"

"Actually, Brandon, it's fine," Jasmine said, tugging on his arm. "We have many people to talk to, and if she needs to finish her show before she can help us, then we're going to let her finish her show."

"But--"

"We have a lot of things we need to do," Jasmine reminded him. She looked back up at the skater. "I know you can't come back to the trailer, but could I ask just a couple more questions?"

"Of course. The Witz kids will handle the set-up just fine. They've been doing this since they put on their first pair of skates."

"What did you just call them?"

Annette's eyes widened. "Oh! You cannot tell them we call them that. They can't know about that."

"What exactly can't they know?" Jasmine asked, pencil in the same ready position.

Annette sighed. "You aren't going to like this."

"I think I'll like it better than not knowing."

"You won't. Charlie and Eve belong to this woman who works in the ice prep chamber. Her name is Georgia, and everyone around here knows that she was having this affair with Mark Witz ever since she has been working here. Everyone knows that Charlie and Eve are his kids, except for the two of them. We call them the Witz kids to poke fun at them, but in all seriousness they cannot hear about this. It would ruin the backstage dynamic."

"So you think their father is the guy we found dead?" Brandon clarified.

"Which is another significant reason they cannot hear about this whole thing. It would stir up way too many emotions in them, and they didn't even think of the guy as a father."

"You have to tell them. You can't keep that a secret, especially now that he's dead."

"Brandon," Jasmine said, shaking her head at him. "That's not why we're here. Annette just gave us some vital evidence which is pointing us towards some new suspects. We're not going to shame her for that."

"Is this guy some sort of trainee?" Annette asked. "You seem to tell him off a lot."

"He's new. I'm really sorry if he's upsetting you."

"No," Annette said with a shrug. "He's fine, I was just worried about how effective you guys would be if you were bickering the entire time."

"We'll work it out. Do you know if Brandy was aware of her husband's potential affair?"

"You don't have to say potential. I honestly don't know. I don't think so, but we didn't speak much about it. We didn't want to risk spilling the truth if she didn't know."

"Okay. We'll try to be gentle if we talk to her. For now, I think we're going to find Georgia and see if she's got anything to say. Do you know where she might be?"

"You've already been backstage, right? There's a trailer on the right-hand side of the backstage area—you'll know it's right because it's the only one that ever keeps the door shut. That'll be the ice management tent, and Georgia should be there."

"Thank you. We'll let you get back to the ice, but I should drop by later to have you walk through the trailer."

"Cool. If you have any trouble finding me, just ask Peter. He knows my entire schedule, so he'll be able to point you in the right direction."

Jasmine thanked her again and headed towards the ice management building. Brandon didn't seem quite as chipper anymore as he went with her.

"You were kind of harsh on me in there."

"You kept saying things that were inappropriate. I'm sorry if I hurt your feelings, but there were things I needed to find out for the investigation."

"I was doing my best."

Jasmine sighed. "I know."

"What?" Luffy exclaimed. "You're going to let him off the hook."

Jasmine stared at Luffy as she spoke her next sentence, as if she was justifying herself to her dog rather than explaining herself to Brandon.

"You're new to this, and everyone starts somewhere. You didn't screw anything up too bad, so it's not a big deal. Just try to let me do most of the talking from now on, okay? I know what I'm doing."

"Fine. Not to sound completely disrespectful, but it's like two-thirty. Could we maybe grab something to eat really quickly?"

Luffy's mouth watered at the mention of food. He remembered the comment before about all the bacon-based food that they sold. He already imagined what Jasmine would get for him. Maybe, if he was lucky, Jasmine would get an entire meal for him, rather than feed him bits and pieces of hers. Dreams came true occasionally.

"Alright. We can grab some food before the next interview."

As they started walking towards the tents where they sold food, Jasmine suddenly stopped in her tracks. Luffy instinctively knew what was happening, but Brandon looked confused. He walked towards her and asked if she was alright, but Luffy could already tell that she was too deep into it to make it out. There was nothing nearby that she could hold on to, and even as she tried every trick she had used in the past, Jasmine couldn't fight back.

As Jasmine clenched her fists, her eyes shut and all at once she fell backwards into Brandon's arms.

CHAPTER 5

J asmine was cold. It was the first sensation she was aware of, even before she opened her eyes. She felt as though she was freezing to death.

When she looked around, the room seemed almost to spin. There was ice everywhere, on every wall, and the way it reflected and refracted light in many unpredictable directions made Jasmine feel dizzy. She put out a hand to steady herself, but all she touched, was more ice.

Then, suddenly, a door appeared. There was too much light, too much color. Jasmine couldn't see anything in the doorway until the door was shut again, replacing itself instantly with a solid wall full of ice. The only difference was that now, standing in front of the door, was a person wearing a thick gray suit and a gas mask. They looked like an astronaut, or like some kind of scientist in a hazmat suit. Jasmine tried her best to make out their features, but no matter how hard she tried she could not bring them into focus.

"Calm down," the figure said, and his voice seemed to swim around her, coming from every direction at once. It echoed around the space just like the light did, and Jasmine was moments away from feeling nauseous. Never had she felt so horribly trapped or so desperate to get out of a situation. She felt her mouth open, as if she had screamed, but she could not tell if any sound passed her lips before it was all gone with a jolt.

The warmth of Brandon's arms replaced the coldness in her vision. He was holding her upright, and as the world came rushing back, she realized that he must have caught her when the vision had pulled her under. She straightened herself, pulling away from him and adjusting her coat. It wasn't any colder than it had been before her vision, but the feeling felt so much more sinister now.

"Are you okay?"

At the same time, Luffy asked: "What did you see?"

She could explain the vision to Luffy soon. She knew Brandon would freak out if she didn't give him some kind of explanation, so she focused on his question first. "I'm fine. I just got lightheaded, that's all."

Brandon frowned. "I think you passed out. Should we take you to a doctor?"

"Honestly, I'm good," she said, hoping that he would take her word for it. "I think perhaps I just need something to eat."

"Okay," Brandon said, hesitantly. When they walked towards the food stands, he stayed closer to Jasmine than he had before her vision. She could tell that he was still really worried about her, and she cursed herself for not being more prepared. It wasn't as if this was the first time she had seen flashes of the future, and with the murder nearby she should have expected one to come on, eventually. She couldn't keep being this careless.

"What was in the vision?" Luffy asked again as they walked. "Did you see any clues?"

Jasmine shot him a look to convey that it was a conversation to have later. Part of the reason was Brandon being there; but if she was being honest, there was a part of her that didn't want to talk about it. The experience had been terrifying, and she wasn't sure she could do it justice with her words, or to relive what she had just seen. She knew she would have to deal with it at some point, but for now food seemed like a better alternative.

The carnival tried very hard to incorporate holiday themed offerings into the traditional food they served up. There were gingerbread flavored churros and giant turkey legs as a holiday feast. Even the caramel apples had festive sprinkles embedded in.

Brandon bought the food, bringing Jasmine a turkey leg that was altogether too big for her to eat and a full mug of hot chocolate.

"I thought you might need protein," he explained. "And we've been outside basically all day, so the cold might take its toll."

"Thanks," she said, pulling off a piece of the turkey leg and tossing it towards Luffy. He had been pouting ever since she hadn't answered his question, but he couldn't resist the smell of food. He chomped down as Jasmine looked up at Brandon. "I'm sorry that a morning trip to the carnival has turned into such a big thing. I can pay you back for the food and everything."

"Don't worry about it," Brandon said, brushing away her concern. "You're solving a murder—I'm here to make sure that goes as smoothly as it can. If that means buying you a turkey leg, it's the absolute least I can do."

"Do you have to get back to the bookshop soon?" Jasmine asked as she ate. She wasn't completely truthful when she attributed her lightheadedness to the lack of food, but she had to admit that it was nice to get some. In between bites, she added: "Don't let me impede your actual work."

"I took the entire day off, in case the carnival was really cool. I can be here for as long as you need me."

At Jasmine's feet, Luffy made a sound that almost resembled a growl. Jasmine looked down at him, confused. Luffy liked Brandon and had even been excited to see him again now that they were back in town. He should have been happy to hear that Brandon was going to be joining them, and when he didn't bother to explain himself, Jasmine assumed he probably still was. She chalked it down to his stomach rumbling or a random sound he made while he ate. She looked back up at Brandon, changing the subject back to the investigation.

"Do you remember seeing any trailers with a closed door? I feel like I would have noticed if one of them was different."

"I don't know. I guess I wasn't paying that much attention."

Jasmine wanted to tell him he should always remain alert, but she didn't want to sound harsh. He was volunteering to help, even when the assistance wasn't as helpful as she would have preferred.

"That's okay. If we still don't see one when we go back there, we can always ask Peter about it. I'm sure he can point us in the right direction."

"I'm pretty sure that all the doors were open," Luffy said from the ground.

"It sounds like there's been some crazy drama going on backstage. I didn't expect we'd get so much information about the personal lives of the employees."

"Personal lives have a lot of emotion tied up in them. When you're thinking about a murder and the motivations for it, emotion is definitely high on the list. So we have to pry sometimes, even if we don't enjoy doing it."

"It still feels kind of..." Brandon paused, trying to think of the right word. "Wrong, I guess. Knowing what people are saying about the father of the children and not telling them makes me feel like we're part of the lie."

"It's tough. But we hardly even know these people. We should try to understand them, but changing the things that go on in their personal lives is way out of our hands."

"Yeah," Brandon said with a breath that wasn't quite a sigh but held the same level of resignation and tone. He seemed to be finished with the subject and went back to eating his food.

Jasmine already ate most of her food, so she sipped at the hot chocolate. It was a little watered down and had the overall impression of being cheap, but just holding the mug helped her feel a tad better after the vision had shaken her up. She tossed what remained of her turkey leg to Luffy and got out her notebook to describe her vision before it slipped her mind.

"What are you doing?" Brandon asked in between bites.

"Just cataloguing some stuff. We've learned a lot already. I don't want to lose any of that."

"That's smart. I already forgot half of the stuff that the medical examiner said."

Jasmine nodded and went back to her writing. When the memory of the vision overwhelmed her, she would pick up the hot chocolate again and draw on its warmth, and by proxy, being safe. With that system in place, she got through a full report of what she had seen and felt. Later, she would go over it with Luffy and see what evidence she might pull from it. For now, documenting it felt like a success.

"Alright," she said, closing the notebook and putting it back in her bag. "You ready to move?"

"Yeah," Brandon said, balling up his trash so he could carry it in a single hand. There was a waste bin down the path he made up his mind to use as they headed back to the backstage area. "Let's go."

Luffy had finished all the meat off the turkey leg and moved on to gnawing on the bone. He seemed to enjoy it, but Jasmine was sure it would make a bad first impression if he carried a bone around during a murder investigation. She wrenched it free from his mouth and put it together with the rest of her trash.

"Hey!" Luffy exclaimed. "You gave that to me! That makes it mine!"

Jasmine reached down to rub his head in the same way she normally did when he needed to calm down, but he backed away from her.

"You're being really mean to me today."

Jasmine sighed. It was more of being practical rather than being intentionally mean, and she wished she could explain that to him without letting everyone know about her unique powers.

"Everything okay?" Brandon asked, concerned.

"I'm good. I was just thinking about the case and the condition the body was in. I've never seen a crime scene like it."

"I'm sure you'll figure it out," Brandon said as they reached the trash can. In the time it had taken them to get there and the brief delay that Luffy's tantrum had caused, someone had emptied the trashcan and they had to wait until he put a fresh bag in. Jasmine turned around to glare at Luffy, but to her surprise, he wasn't following at her heels like he normally did. She looked around with a little more scrutiny, expecting to see him sitting nearby and moping about some perceived slight or staring at the bone she had taken from him. Luffy was nowhere in sight.

"Hey, Brandon, have you seen Luffy?"

"Weren't you wrestling with him over that turkey bone?" Brandon asked, equally puzzled. Luffy had just been there with them a couple of seconds ago, and they hadn't gone nearly far enough for him to have any chance of getting lost. Jasmine remembered the icy prison chamber from her vision and worry that someone had kidnapped Luffy washed all over her.

"Yeah, but I don't see him anymore."

"Don't worry. He won't have gone far."

"Can I help you kids find someone?" the janitor asked, pausing with the fresh bag halfway in the trashcan.

"No, it's okay," Jasmine answered, but Brandon quickly contradicted her.

"My friend's dog kind of disappeared on us. He's a golden retriever, and he always looks like he's smiling. You didn't see him go by, did you? He was just here a second ago."

"I haven't seen him. But I can help you kids find him if you need help."

"We really do," Jasmine admitted. The only reason she hadn't wanted to admit to losing Luffy was the fear of a lecture about keeping her dog on a leash. But the janitor didn't sound like the kind of person who would do that. "His name is Luffy, and I'm Jasmine."

"Hank," the janitor beamed. He was a lot older than most of the people working in the park and seemed to be about the same age as Jasmine's grandparents. As soon as he was done with the trashcan, he walked around the side of the nearest tent. "If your dog was here only a moment ago, my guess is he's still around. There are a lot of corners around here, and when a kid goes missing it's usually just around one of those. I'd reckon it would be the same for any loved ones of the four-legged variety."

He had a good point. Though Luffy was nowhere in sight, there were plenty of places where he could be that were out of sight. Jasmine started peeking around corners and calling after him. A corner wouldn't be able to keep him out of earshot.

"Luffy!" she called, resulting in a few weird looks from the other carnival guests. "Luffy, come back here, this isn't funny."

It wasn't like Luffy to take off by himself, especially without her knowing. Especially since she had gained the ability to communicate with him in words.

The more she looked, the more convinced she became that someone had abducted him. She kept thinking back to Barry Brock and Blackwood Cove's famous scandal. That had been going on for years without anyone finding out, and if someone had swiped Luffy for the same nefarious purposes, they might also get away with it. She couldn't imagine Luffy stuck in such an awful place, and she felt as if she was going to cry.

Brandon seemed to notice her distress, and he put an arm over her shoulder. "Hey, it's going to be okay. This is Luffy we're talking about. He's probably already on his way back here, we just need to give him a minute."

"Right. I'm really worried—there's someone bad here, and now Luffy's on his own, and I feel like it's my fault."

"Whoa, chill. It's not your fault at all. You're amazing with Luffy, and he loves you. If anything happened, which probably isn't the case, you're the last person in the world who should take the blame for it."

Jasmine nodded and tried to pull herself together. Luffy was smart and strong, and he could fend for himself. They were in the middle of the carnival now, and there was no way to escape without going past countless people. Someone would have seen him if something bad had happened, and they would have stopped it. Brandon was probably right—the carnival was probably just too distracting for Luffy. The smells alone would have been enough to lead him away.

"I don't see him," Hank said, walking over to them. "I've got to get back to my rounds, but I'll keep my eye out for him. I'll tell the others who work here too, to get a bunch of eyes on this. He won't get far, I promise you ma'am."

"Thank you."

"In the meantime, get back to your fun. This carnival isn't here for long, and I wouldn't want you to miss out because your dog got a bit too excited. If we find this 'Luffy', I'll get them to make an announcement."

Jasmine was torn. On one hand, she didn't think she could focus on the case with Luffy missing, and it could take a long time to go after him. On the other hand, she had a responsibility to help the people she had promised to help. There was an interview waiting for her, and if she waited too long, she could miss her chance to talk to the people she needed to talk to. It probably wasn't fair to stake the results of the case on how fast she could find her runaway, and it wouldn't look good to any potential future clients.

"We probably should get back to the case," Brandon said, deciding for her. "There are going to be lots of people looking for Luffy. Our extra eyes wouldn't even make a difference."

"You think so?"

"Of course. It's like when a person goes missing from a town. The police stay where they are and do the investigating, and the town themselves put together a search party to do the work of finding the person."

"I guess."

"If anything bad happened, which I still don't think is likely, it probably is connected to the case, right? I mean, what are the chances of there being more than one rotten apple in a place this small?"

"I guess."

"So solving the case faster might be all you need to do to get Luffy back faster. And if this has nothing to do with the case, that means Luffy's just begging bacon off strangers, or mesmerized by a couple of ice sculptures that look like giant lollipops."

He made a good point, and Jasmine agreed to go to the interview. They walked to the back of the park, and this time let themselves through the gate to go backstage. They got a couple of strange looks from guests who could easily tell they weren't staff, but that only lasted a few seconds before they were out of view.

Again they found themselves looking at the trailers. Lustbader had marked off the one where the body had been found as a crime scene, and there were a few more people hanging around, but otherwise little had changed. Jasmine looked around for a trailer with a door closed and spotted one furthest to the left.

"That's got to be where we're heading," Jasmine surmised, pointing it out to Brandon.

"I guess there was a trailer with a door closed like Annette said."

Jasmine still wasn't fully convinced. The trailer in question had the door closed, but it didn't mean it would always be closed, or that it had been the last time they were there. She was also fairly certain Annette had said the trailer in question would be on the right of the backstage area, and finding it on the left was not adding all that much credibility to her story. She grabbed her notebook and jotted the inconsistency down for later. It seemed like what someone involved in the carnival would have known.

When they got to the trailer, Jasmine knocked on the door. There was no response, so Brandon stepped up and did the same, but with more force. Still nothing.

"I guess no one's home," Brandon said, looking around. "They probably just keep the door shut to keep people from poking around."

"Or to keep the cold in," Jasmine mused. Given the other open doors, it didn't exactly seem likely their need for privacy would start and end with the ice management area.

"It's like 30 degrees out here."

"And they found the body at a lower temperature than that. It doesn't really matter why the door is shut. If no one is here, we need to find someone else to talk to. I know it's probably too early to talk to the widow, but I think we'd be able to learn a lot."

"Right. We can go right to the source that way," Brandon said, with a nod betraying too much confidence. Jasmine had almost forgotten he was tagging along for the interviews and wondered if he was ready.

She was just starting to think of alternatives, when someone came up behind them. It was Paul, the man who had so graciously offered to watch after Luffy from before. He had traded in the sleigh skids for wheels that seemed to be altogether too thick for the rather minimal chair. It took Jasmine a while to piece together what they were for, to help steady the chair in the grass and mud that made up the backstage area.

"What are you two doing back here? And where's that dog of yours?"

Jasmine gave him a brief explanation of the events that had led them there, ending with the closed door to the empty trailer.

"Oh... that's definitely not empty. Georgia is almost always in there, and I don't think I've ever seen her leave during work hours."

"But we--" Brandon started, but Paul was already shaking his head.

"You knocked on the door a few times and didn't get any answer. I heard you, but Georgia probably didn't. The equipment can be pretty loud."

"So how do we get in?" Jasmine asked. "We really need to talk to her to confirm a few facts."

"I can help," Paul said, and he pulled out a cell phone. He hit a few buttons, then held it up to his ear. After about thirty seconds, he started nodding his head. "Hey Georgia, I've got a couple kids out here who want to talk to you."

Jasmine preferred being labeled as a private detective than a kid, but she would take what she could get. She watched him nod a couple more times to whatever was being said on the other side of the line before ending the call.

"Give her a second. She needs to take off her gloves, and then she'll be right out."

"Great," Jasmine said, looking back at her notebook and prepared her questions mentally. "Thanks for your help."

"Again," Brandon added.

"Not a problem. Let me know if you need anything else for the case. I've got connections all over the carnival."

He rolled off, having to put a good deal of work into moving the chair across the ground. Jasmine wondered if she should try to help him, but another employee of the carnival ran over and gave Paul a hand as if it was an automatic reflex.

After about two more minutes, the door to the trailer opened. Jasmine, who was already feeling a tad chilly, was hit with a blast of cold air. The figure standing in the doorway was dressed in a dark black suit that covered her entire body, revealing only her head and hands. She had dark hair pulled into a ponytail, but most of it was trying to escape into a layer of frizz above it. She didn't have any makeup on, but there was an edge to her looks that would have made it easy to think otherwise.

"Hi. You must be the two that Paul called about. Where did he run off to?"

Jasmine nodded to where Paul was being pushed in his chair towards a different trailer.

"That's a pity. It's always good to see him. I would have liked to say hi."

Georgia looked at Brandon and Jasmine from top to toe thoroughly. When she made it back to their faces, she tilted her head to the side. "I'm usually pretty good at this, but I've got nothing. What are you two here for? Jobs? An interview for the school paper?"

"Interview is almost right," Jasmine answered, trying to dismiss the insinuation that she looked like a high-schooler. "I'm a private investigator, and I wanted to ask you a couple of questions."

"About Mark?"

"Yes, that's right."

"Oh, come on. I can see the police tape from here, and I know exactly what rumors were flying around. I knew it wouldn't be long before the questions came my way. You can ask me whatever you want, but I have work to do, so I'd really prefer it if you would do it in here."

Georgia stepped back into her trailer, but Jasmine hesitated, remembering her vision. It seemed like an especially foolish move to step into a cold, enclosed box with someone in an alien-like suit, when she knew exactly what those conditions would eventually do to her. She especially didn't like the door shutting behind her.

"Come on," Brandon tapped her shoulder. "Work to do, remember?"

Jasmine took a deep breath and stepped into the trailer, but she couldn't shake the feeling of discomfort. She pulled her coat closer in on her body, trying to generate as much warmth out of it as she could. She really didn't want to feel anything like the cold that had plagued her in her vision.

When they made it all the way into the trailer, she felt a little better. The cold was harsh, but the room itself looked nothing like she had seen in her vision. The floor was coated in a fairly thick layer of ice like she remembered, but thankfully that was all. A snowlike layer of frozen water coated the walls, similar to the frost you would normally see accumulating on the walls of a poorly kept freezer. It didn't reflect light in the same way the ice in Jasmine's vision had, and strangely enough the room itself seemed too small to fit the bill. After such a claustrophobic vision, Jasmine wouldn't have thought such a thing possible. As Brandon stepped in after her, she calmed herself down almost entirely.

The place she saw in her vision was not the same as the trailer she was in.

"I would offer you a seat, but you came at a pretty bad time. Nothing's frozen over for the day yet," Georgia said. She nodded at several low basins that looked like oversized baking pans. One was visibly full to the brim with water, but the others seemed at least partially through freezing over. The ones that Georgia had gestured towards were thin, but there were several similar containers scattered around the room of all different shapes and sizes. Now that she was looking around more closely, Jasmine noticed a few odd shapes thrown in among the finished blocks, as if some of them had melted.

"That's okay," Jasmine said, turning back to Georgia. "We really appreciate you taking the time to talk with us."

"I know you aren't technically the cops, but they'll be here soon too. I'll have to explain myself at some point, anyway. I may as well start now."

"Well... still, thank you," Jasmine said, getting out her notebook. "Is it okay if we start now?"

"Yeah, no problem. Do the two of you want goggles?"

"Goggles?" Brandon asked, eyes widening. He was going through the stages of fear that Jasmine had gone through as he realized they were trapped in a small frozen box. And with them, a suspect in the murder of a partially frozen man.

"I'm going to be chopping some ice, and some shards might fly off. You know what, you don't know nearly enough about this to make your own decisions. I'll get you some, before Peter sues me over a bit of stray water."

Georgia turned her back on them and reached behind some containers. When she pulled her arm back, there were two pairs of goggles looped around her wrist by the straps.

"Put them on," she said, handing them to Brandon and Jasmine. "I wouldn't want to blind a private eye."

She seemed rather pleased with her own joke, and Jasmine and Brandon might have smiled if the situation had been different. She grabbed a small hatchet off the wall and seized a full container. Jasmine could just see over the edge and noticed that this one looked completely frozen.

"What are you going to do with that?" Jasmine asked. The availability of the hatchet concerned her, even though she knew that it wasn't the weapon that had caused Mark's death. It felt convenient to have a hatchet so easily within reach when you were being investigated. Jasmine wondered if the cold was allowing paranoia to set in.

"Oh, I just need to take off the corners. This one is pretty thin, so I'm thinking it will probably make a nice pedestal. It's going to have to be a lot more trouble than this if we want that to work out."

Using the back of her axe, she tapped around the outside edge of the container. She was firm but did not put much force into it, hitting it with the same confidence of someone tapping the top of a soda can to keep the fizz from rushing at them too quickly.

"Pedestal?"

"Yeah, like a base. You've seen the ice sculptures, right? You can't always see it beneath the snow, but they've all got some solid ice underneath them. It keeps them sturdier, and it makes them a lot easier to transport."

"Those sculptures are yours?" Jasmine asked, following the

words to their logical conclusion.

"Yeah. What did you think I did in here?"

Jasmine shrugged. "I wasn't sure, but I figured the sculptures were prepared ahead of time."

"They melt a bit and warp even in great conditions. I try to replace one or two of them every day so that the trail looks fresh."

"They looked amazing when we were over there earlier," Brandon added. Jasmine had nearly forgotten that he was there at all, which she supposed was a good sign. At the very least, it meant he was letting her take the lead.

"Thanks. Opening day is always the best."

As fascinating as the conversation was, Jasmine needed to know things about the case. She steered the topic back casually.

"So, you said you knew people were spreading rumors about you?" Jasmine asked, hoping it would lead Georgia to share more about herself.

"Of course I did. It's not like it was a well-kept secret. Everyone in the carnival knew about it, and it was a popular topic. I think it made them feel like they were a part of something."

"Did you ever try to contradict the rumors?"

"Oh, at first. Mostly for Brandy's sake. I didn't want people to think Mark was leaving her, but the only time I talked to her about it, she seemed pretty confident he had done nothing. If it was just going to be about me, I didn't mind so much."

"So was the rumor true? Is Mark Witz the father of your kids?"

"I bet you'd like to know, wouldn't you?" Georgia said with a bit of a laugh, shaking her head. "No. He isn't the father of my kids."

"Then who--" Brandon started to ask, before Jasmine cut him off. She didn't want Brandon to pry too far and make Georgia uncomfortable.

"Do you know why people thought he was?"

"Yeah, of course. A while back, I let my certification lapse, so I couldn't load the liquid nitrogen onto the trailer. Peter tried to replace me with a newer sculptor, but he couldn't get anyone willing to work at my output levels. So, he ended up hiring a liquid nitrogen specialist for a couple of months while I got the paperwork filled out."

"And Mark had an affair with the liquid nitrogen specialist?" Brandon pipped in.

"No, but they were friends. Turns out they knew each other from high school or something. Mark kept popping into my trailer to talk to him, and they would chat for most of the night. People saw Mark coming out of my trailer and assumed that he had been with me. That's when the rumors started flying."

"Why didn't he just explain about the friend?"

"Oh, Mark didn't know what was being said. He's good at convincing people, and I think everyone knew that if he found out about the rumors, they would have to end. He's clueless sometimes, but I think people were trying to keep him out of the loop on this one."

"So why didn't you explain?" Brandon asked.

"I mentioned him a few times, back when this was being passed around in whispers, but by the time things got really intense, the guy wasn't even around anymore. No one except Peter and Mark had even really noticed that he was there. And so, when I started blaming the rumors on someone that was conveniently not around, it made me look even more guilty."

"So if the rumors were false, were you ever resentful of Mark for not doing more to stop them? Or for his role in putting you in this position?"

"Not really. I mean, I guess I was a little annoyed at first. It was all new, and I felt like that was all anyone was ever going to think about me. But you know, he really didn't have any idea what was going on. Even the people who spread the rumor eventually realized that I was more than just the other woman to some guy they thought they knew. It's hard to bear any resentment towards him for that."

"Okay. Do you know of anyone who might have felt a little resentful?"

"I mean, normally you would think his wife, right? But she's known about the rumors for a long time, so I don't think anything would have changed recently. Besides, like I said before, she never really believed that he had done anything."

"That's good to know. You've been a tremendous help."

"Good. Could you help me with this?"

"With what?" Jasmine asked, looking up from her notebook. Georgia's hands were braced against the side of the container she had been hammering away at a moment before.

"Just grab the other end," Georgia said, and Jasmine did as she was told. The surface of the ice stung her hands, and before she knew what was happening, Georgia was lifting her end of the container.

"Lift it up," Georgia instructed, and Jasmine gave it her best try. It wasn't easy, and she looked back at Brandon for help. He quickly stepped forward and added his strength to hers.

"Amateurs," Georgia said, shaking her head. "We're going to lower your left side down to the ground and lift the right side."

Jasmine expected a count of sorts, but Georgia was already starting to tip the whole thing over. With Brandon's help, she tipped her side too, and they slowly turned the container upside down. Jasmine couldn't help but think about how lucky they were that the ice hadn't slipped out of the frame while they were trying to flip it over. She couldn't know for sure, but she guessed Georgia would not have taken kindly to that result.

"Okay, thanks. That usually takes me... well, less time on my own but it is more of a strain on my arms, I think."

Jasmine wasn't really sure if it was a token of appreciation, but she took it as one. The ice block had been heavier than pretty much anything she had tried to lift recently, and even doing as much as she had managed there had been quite the feat.

"You're welcome," Brandon said, taking a deep breath and shaking out his arms a little to Jasmine's surprise. After all his hours lugging around books for the Book Nook, she figured he wouldn't have any problems lifting a bit of ice.

"Did you guys have any more questions?" Georgia asked. With a few swift taps from the back of her axe, she loosened the metal frame that held the ice from what had once been the bottom, and she pulled the metal away completely. "I usually put on an audiobook when I tackle this part, and it's going to be a bit of a hassle if I have to take off the gloves and set everything up again."

"I think that's enough to go on for now," Jasmine said, and as she prepared to leave, she glimpsed something by the door. It was a big trash bin, the kind you would see in a cafeteria, or somewhere with many people and a very low bar for how things looked. The trash can itself was pretty innocuous, but it was about halfway full with thin shards of ice. She wouldn't have even questioned something like that in a place like she was in, except she had seen a shard an awful lot like the ones in the trailer currently holding a dead body. "Actually, what's this?"

"It's waste. I melt it down at the end of the day and add it back in to be frozen. It's better if it thaws completely first though, just so that the finished ice will be nice and uniform."

"Does anyone else have access to this stuff?" Jasmine asked, picking up a single shard and balancing it in her palm.

"Anyone, if they ask for it. It's just ice. If you stick around, you can both put those goggles to good use and find out where that stuff comes from."

"No, that's okay," Jasmine said, taking off the goggles and handing them back. "I was wondering if anyone has come through here recently who might have picked up one of these."

"Well, if you're looking for a thief, you might try Rick. He went through here the other day, and he's got a pretty poor reputation for swiping things that he probably shouldn't. I wouldn't be surprised if he took a few pieces hoping it would mess me up."

"Rick," Jasmine repeated the name, turning to Brandon. "I think we may have already met him. Over at the Ferris wheel."

"Yes, I remember him. He was that teenager who was not excited about Luffy being around."

"I don't know who Luffy is, but a teenager not being excited about something sounds an awful lot like you've got the right guy. Now, staying or going? I need to start on this."

"Going," Jasmine answered, grabbing the door handle. It was made of metal and had accumulated its own layer of snowy frost that coated the walls. Her hand melted away a little of it, revealing a layer of solid ice beneath. She tossed the door open as quickly as she could to get away from that extra touch of cold and stomped down the steps. She would never have guessed that the outside air as it was today would feel warm to her, but as she was stepping out of the trailer that was exactly what she thought. It was solidly ten degrees warmer outside than it had been in the trailer, and yet it was still below freezing.

"Shut the door!" Georgia called after them. Jasmine made sure that it latched before she walked away.

"I did better this time, right?" Brandon asked.

"Yeah. You seemed a little too invested in the rumors, but other than that you were good."

"I think it's relevant. If the kid didn't belong to Mark, but the actual father got wind that people were saying so, it might have plunged him into a jealous rage. I think that's worth investigating."

It was far from the worst idea that Brandon had shared all day, and now Jasmine felt a little guilty for stopping his line of questioning. She had been so caught up in making sure he didn't screw things up that she hadn't been able to focus on the possibility that he was being helpful.

"We can ask her about it next time we talk. For now, I want to find Hank and check in about Luffy. I'm not convinced we would have been able to hear any announcement through all the ice in there."

"Right. Where do you think he would be?"

Jasmine wasn't sure, but she was prepared to walk the entire park to find out if she needed to. It was taking pretty much all of her self-control not to go after him already. Luffy was her partner and soulmate, and now that they were separated, it was impossible to think of anything else. She hadn't even gotten the chance to tell him about the vision, so he wouldn't know to be careful around enclosed icy spaces and people with strange suits. Deep down, Jasmine hoped they weren't too late to save Luffy.

CHAPTER 6

While Jasmine was worrying about Luffy, her dog was thinking about her too, with significantly less affection.

Luffy loved Jasmine, but she had not been treating him like a proper partner at all during this case. Everything had been about Brandon and making sure he didn't think she was crazy. There had always been rules in place about when they could hold a proper conversation, but they had never been as restrictive as they had been lately. Usually, they would have plenty of time to talk about things as they walked from place to place, and Jasmine would make a point of finding a place and time to tell him about any vision she might have had. Now Luffy could barely get a word in edge-wise—he hadn't told Jasmine yet about the smell of blood or the footprint or the conversation he had overheard.

He had decided, after Jasmine had taken the turkey bone away from him, that he would not put up with it. He loved Jasmine, and he would still play fetch with her and walk her home and do everything an obedient dog would do, but he would not be her detective sidekick anymore. Not if she wasn't going to listen to him or give him enough credit.

Instead, Luffy was striking out on his own. He was going to prove to Jasmine that he had detective skills worth listening to by solving the case on his own. Maybe then Jasmine would let him work with her again in the way he had used to. He was sick of being treated like a passenger on the murder train.

The first place his investigation took him to was Brandy. Luffy knew that she was a widow, and that she didn't like him, but he was not going to let human traditions impede his investigation.

The problem was, Brandy was hard to find. He sniffed around all the trailers that he could find, even sneaking into some of them, but he couldn't find any trace of her. He remembered her mentioning someone named Danny in the phone call, but he had no way of knowing which of the people hanging around backstage were Daniel, or if it was even any of them at all. He couldn't ask around like Jasmine could, and even his sense of smell was pretty useless once he got too far away. He was losing hope when he got to the last of the trailers. He had saved it for last because the door was shut, and he didn't know if he could beg his way in or not. He was usually pretty good at getting humans to open doors for him, but the ones here had been giving him increasingly suspicious looks. There weren't a lot of dogs around to begin with, if there were any others at all, and he figured it wouldn't be too much longer before someone decided he had to be lost and dragged him back into the main carnival area. He figured that time, which had never been long, would shorten significantly if he made a fuss.

As he was walking up to the door and starting to debate whether it was worth an attempt despite the risk, there was a sound from inside. The latch holding the door shut came undone and pushed open. It was instinct that pushed Luffy away from the sound of the door opening, but once he saw who was coming out of the trailer, he was glad that he had ducked around the corner and as far out of sight as he could get. Jasmine and Brandon walked out of the trailer, shutting the door behind them and talking in hushed voices that Luffy couldn't quite hear. They didn't look in his direction at all and marched forward towards some goal that Luffy didn't know about. It stung a little that they weren't looking for him, but he had been the one to abandon them, so he couldn't be too mad about it.

He watched them walk away before deciding that whatever was in this trailer was not something he needed. He could solve this case without retracing their steps.

Luffy didn't want to go straight back into the common area between the trailers for fear that one of the workers would decide that he had been hanging around for too long. He wasn't quite sure what lead to follow next, but he was pretty sure he could get there from behind the trailers as easily as he would from the front. He walked around the trailer that Jasmine and Brandon had just left, and was surprised to see several large, metal tanks. They were about the same size as a human being, and looked like they had big lids on the top with a lot of latches to keep them secure. Luffy wasn't sure what they could be or why they would be piled up outside the trailer, but he thought it might be a clue. He walked up to the barrels and nudged one with his nose to see how heavy it was. It didn't budge, but he felt like he could move it if he was a little stronger—Jasmine could probably tip it and maybe even push it along, and he wouldn't be surprised if someone like Brandon could lift the whole thing. Luffy didn't know if the barrels were clues, but they were definitely interesting. He tried to remember them as he moved on.

His primary goal was still to find Brandy, but he was steadily losing hope in doing so. He decided he should try to listen in on some of the conversations that the employees had. Jasmine could ask them direct questions, but Luffy's ability to observe them when they thought they were mostly alone might prove even more valuable.

There was a fairly large group of people hanging out around the bed of a flatbed truck. Some were sitting on it, others stood on the ground, and even more people were perched on patio furniture they had set up at the top of the truck. Luffy recognized Paul from the ice slides, which meant that Paul would probably recognize him and he needed to stay out of sight. While everyone was busy laughing at a joke Luffy didn't hear, he covered the distance between himself and the group and took up a new hiding place beneath the truck. He could hear everything, but he didn't think anyone could see him.

"You know, there's a good chance that this will put the company under," someone said, and Luffy quickly realized the flaw in his plan was that he couldn't tell who was talking. He hadn't recognized anyone other than Paul, and it would have been nice to have the chance to put faces together with comments in case someone said something suspicious.

"It's not exactly a good look," someone else agreed. "Hard to sell the best time of your life to people when your employees can't even hold on to their lives."

"I think we'll make it out okay," Paul said. Luffy could recognize his voice, and the bottom of Paul's wheelchair was distinctive enough that he could figure out where he was. "The bad press will balance out with there being press to begin with. I'll bet the free advertising we get from people freaking out about the murder brings in just as many guests as the fear scares away."

"Maybe," someone else said. "People can be kind of dumb sometimes."

"Don't say that like it's a bad thing. Dumb tourists are what keep this company afloat to begin with."

"So who do you guys think it is?"

"I don't know. Do you really believe it's one of us?"

"I heard his blood was drained like the victim of a vampire. Isn't that Rick kid into some weird stuff like that?"

"No, that was like a year ago, and I think it was just a TV show he was into," Paul said.

"Still. If that's what you find entertaining, it's not a tremendous leap to carrying it out, is it?"

"It kind of is," Paul answered. "I mean, I enjoy watching track and field on TV, but I'm not leaping out of my chair to go for a run. I think it would be quite the leap if I managed that."

"Alright, fine. Maybe the kid's just weird. Who do you think did it?"

There was a silence before Paul spoke, as if everyone was waiting to see what he could have to say.

"I think... I mean, I don't think it's any of us, but since the police are saying it has to be... I'd guess it's one of the ballet women. Annette or Henrietta. They've always been cruel to him."

"Annette? Really? She's a sweetheart!"

"Henrietta too!"

"Yes, right, they're both amazing. Why on earth would they kill Mark Witz? Better yet, how on earth would they kill him? They barely weigh more than the man's kids."

"It has got to be Georgia. She's got the muscle mass for it and enough of a motive to make sense."

"Doesn't she own an axe?"

"I heard it was a hammer, but yeah, definitely weapon potential there."

"And that ice box... didn't someone say something about the body being chilled?"

"Yeah, I heard that too."

"I think he froze to death. Isn't that what they're saying?"

"No, he was just frozen solid when they found him. Like a popsicle."

"That has Georgia written all over it."

"What about his wife? Maybe she found out about the Witz kids? That's a better motive."

"Better motive, way less opportunity. I think opportunity counts for more in court, doesn't it?"

"How should I know?"

"It doesn't matter either way. Brandy doesn't have motive. She's closer to that Danny guy these days than she ever was with Mark."

Luffy had been just about ready to give up on the conversation, but his ears perked up at the mention of Danny. He remembered the name from the phone call.

"Yeah, who is that guy? I've been hearing a lot about him lately, but I've never seen him."

"He doesn't work here."

"No, he does, he just isn't big on socializing. I talked to Peter about it one time."

"Who does he even stay with?"

"Most nights? Brandy."

"Yeah, but like officially."

"Who knows? No one here."

"Has anyone even seen him? Is this a real guy, or someone that

Brandy made up so she didn't look like the one being cheated on anymore?"

"I've seen him! He and Brandy were like thirty steps back into the forest and they were smoking. I only saw them from the back, but I remembered thinking they were going to burn the place down."

"Peter would probably just turn the snow machines on full blast. He could cover a city with those in ten minutes if he had the chance."

They went on talking about Peter, but Luffy had gotten the information he wanted. If Brandy hung out behind the trailers in the little forest, she might be there now. He had seen her walk in the other direction after her phone call, but that had been several hours ago now and she could easily have doubled back while Luffy had been with Jasmine. Even if she wasn't, Luffy could look in the forest for signs she had been there before. Considering all the evidence they had found behind the trailer was closest to the forest, it would be a big deal just to know if anyone had a habit of hanging out back there. Luffy ducked out from under the flatbed truck to go see what was going on.

"Hey, can someone stop that dog?" asked an unfamiliar voice. "I think I know who it belongs to."

Luffy tried to scramble away before anyone could get to him, but a woman in a requisite blue sweater grabbed him as he tried to go by. She held him a little too tightly as he squirmed, which made it both impossible to escape and very uncomfortable not to.

"I know that dog," Paul said, rolling a few inches forward. "He belongs to a couple of sweet kids. I think they were on their first date."

Date? Luffy hadn't heard about Jasmine and Brandon dating since before she had gone to college, and even then it had only been a one-sided attraction. He didn't think anything had started up between them since they had been back, but he supposed it would explain why she had only been paying attention to Brandon lately and never to himself.

"Yeah, I met them too," said an old man who Luffy didn't

recognize. "They were freaking out because they couldn't find this poor guy. I promised I'd keep an eye out for him and told everyone on shift to do the same."

"You should have told the people not on shift," someone said. "We've been watching that dog run around unsupervised for the better part of an hour."

"Well, at least he's going to get back to his right home. Gina, hand him off to Paul, we'll go find the kids."

They manhandled Luffy in Paul's direction until he was on his lap. Luffy might have been able to get away if he had fought the transition harder, but he worried about hurting Paul more than he did about the others. He had been nice to Jasmine and nice to him when he had offered to watch Luffy while Brandon and Jasmine enjoyed the ice slides. Besides, he could just run away again once he was back with Jasmine.

Luffy expected the men who had taken him to walk around aimlessly, trying to figure out where Jasmine was and therefore where he belonged, but they moved with a sense of purpose he hadn't been expecting. Aside from a slight detour to put the runners back on Paul's chair, they didn't seem to stop at all, and it wasn't until they got to the ticket booth at the front of the carnival that Luffy understood why. They weren't taking him straight to Jasmine, as he had been expecting. They were going to get Jasmine to come to him.

They made an announcement on the overhead intercom system about a lost dog and waited for a response. Luffy expected it to take a while, as Jasmine was probably wrapping up whatever interview she was in the middle of and discussing it with Brandon. The last thing he expected was for Jasmine to dash across the snow to him, eyes alight with relief.

"You found him," she said, out of breath. Jasmine helped Luffy down from Paul's lap and gave him a big hug. "Thank you, so much, I was seriously worried about him."

"There was nothing to be worried about," said the older man who Luffy had matched with a name. "He was just wandering around backstage the whole time. Some of the workers saw him, but I hadn't thought to alert people not on shift, so they didn't bring him in. I probably could have had him back to you in half the time if I'd thought about that."

"Well, I'm just glad he's safe," Jasmine said, looking down at Luffy. "Where were you, buddy? I looked back, and you weren't there."

Anyone watching them would assume she was talking to Luffy in the same manner that a child might talk to a doll, with no expectation of a real response. In reality, of course, there was a genuine curiosity behind her words, and Luffy felt compelled to explain himself. He didn't think Jasmine would be happy that he had run off to solve the case without her, especially considering how little he had dug up. Seeing how happy she was to see him safe made him feel loved and appreciated again, which had been the whole reason he had felt the need to branch off on his own in the first place.

"I was going to solve the case on my own. I wanted to go check on Brandy."

Jasmine's expression went from confusion to something that looked like anger, but before Luffy could say anything more, Brandon came jogging.

"You just kind of left," he said, shaking his head at Jasmine. "I tried to explain to Rick that you had important things to do, but he really didn't like us to begin with. It's going to be tricky to set up another interview with him."

"I had to come get Luffy. I was worried about him."

"You knew he was safe as soon as they made the announcement. Could you not have taken five minutes to explain the situation to Rick before you moved on?"

Jasmine opened her mouth to refute him, but a bit of drama interrupted them near the entrance. The sound of something slamming against something else drew their attention over to one of the entrance booths. Peter stood in front of the entrance, looking like he was barely containing his anger.

"Don't you need more evidence to do this? I think you're supposed to know pretty much for sure, right?"

Jasmine leaned her head around the side of the booth to see who Peter was trying to refuse entry to. It surprised her to see Lustbader standing there, looking altogether more like a police officer than Jasmine had ever seen him look. He was wearing a uniform that looked as though it had been specially cleaned and pressed for the very occasion, and he was holding a paper with enough text on it to look vaguely important.

"I have all the evidence I need. I would really like for you to let me through now. I don't want there to be any trouble between us."

"Can't you at least walk around the back of the carnival? I'm sure you know where you're going, I showed you the way in just this morning. I'd really like to keep this issue out of the eyes of the guests. We don't want them freaking out."

"I'm happy to use the back entrance when I'm merely searching for clues. Right now, I'm here to take someone into custody. The longer I have to wait to do that, the longer a dangerous person is out in the world where they can cause harm."

At the mention of taking someone into custody, Jasmine walked towards them, completely forgetting about Luffy and whatever drama had been going on with him. Luffy reluctantly followed. At least this time she was ignoring him for something interesting and important.

"Sheriff," Jasmine greeted, feeling as if the occasion required more formality than she would otherwise use. "Did I hear you were taking someone into custody?"

"I am. Or at least I'm doing my level best to. Peter here seems to take issue with the idea."

"I'm happy to let you take whoever you need to into custody, I'm just asking you to be more discreet. You of all people understand how important it is to keep everyone calm. Mass panics can cause--"

"Peter," Lustbader said, giving him a harsh look. "I'm not trying to cause a fight in the middle of your carnival. I'm asking to cut through the main area so I can get where I need to be a little faster."

"Peter, you should probably just let him through," Jasmine suggested, then turned her gaze to Lustbader. "Who are you taking into custody?"

"Brandy Witz," Lustbader replied, offering no other explanation. He fixed an unmoving glare on Peter until the man relented and moved out of the way. The sheriff marched into the carnival with purpose, his heavy footsteps seeming to compact the snow as much as the hundreds of people who had come before him combined. Jasmine hurried after him, trying to put together what she could to explain why he would arrest Brandy.

"The widow?" she asked when she had caught up with him.

"Yes. I've run her records, and she has a criminal past, including an armed robbery. It was enough to make me take a second look at her, and when May called to say she'd found a partial print on Mark's neck, Brandy's were the first prints I had her check. We got a match."

"You got a fingerprint?" Jasmine asked, more surprised than she really should have been. The police used fingerprints to track suspects all the time.

"May, the forensic scientist, got a print. It was only a partial, and it was tricky to lift off the skin, but the cold helped to preserve it. We were able to match it to some records we had on file for Brandy Witz."

Jasmine didn't have access to fingerprint evidence, and she couldn't dispute it. Her mind was already spinning with ways that Brandy Witz's fingerprint could have ended up on her husband's neck, but no wild speculation about the case was going to get Brandy out of trouble. Jasmine wished she had some kind of evidence to know whether Brandy was actually guilty or being falsely accused. She hadn't even talked to the widow since she had kicked Luffy out of the trailer.

"Are you sure it's her?"

"I wouldn't be arresting her if I wasn't," Lustbader said without stopping his walk.

Jasmine slowed, letting Lustbader get ahead of her. Luffy and Brandon soon caught up to her.

"So I guess the case is over," she said, not really believing her own words. Peter had hired her, and only he could really say when her work was done. If he didn't trust the arrest, which was clear from his reaction at the front gate, she could stay on to find out more about the case. Jasmine walked back to him and let him know of his options.

"Oh..." Peter said, looking around as if it embarrassed him to talk about the crime in a public area. "I really don't know who it was. If the police think it's Brandy and they want to take her away for it, I'm fine with that."

"What about all those things you were saying about him needing more evidence?"

"I mean, I care about evidence, but I don't really know what he has on her. I didn't want him marching through the carnival and scaring everyone, but it's clear that he's going to do that anyway. "

"So you're not going to fight him on this at all?"

"Frankly, he's gotten the issue out of my hair. I'm going to focus on my carnival and making sure my guests see a good place to have fun, and not the site of this town's most recent murder."

Jasmine must have made a particularly discontented face, because Peter reached over and patted her on the back.

"Don't worry. I know you probably hoped to solve this on your own, but I'll pay you whatever you need. I saw you talking to the sheriff a few times, and if you helped get this problem solved, you deserve whatever your hourly rate is."

Jasmine felt really weird about the situation. She trusted Lustbader and knew he wouldn't throw around accusations or arrest anyone that he didn't truly believe belonged in jail. But even knowing that, it was really hard to walk away. It was different this time, as she didn't really have any firsthand knowledge of the person being taken to jail.

Still, Jasmine knew money was important to keep her private eye firm from failing before she could really get off the ground. After a quick negotiation, which felt an awful lot like Peter just agreeing to whatever she asked for, she walked back to Brandon and Luffy.

"I guess that's it," she said, looking between them.

"Cool," Brandon said. "You want to go grab dinner at the diner?"

"That's okay," Jasmine answered, turning to look at Luffy. "I think I'll probably just head home and relax a bit with Luffy. I kind of need to figure out why he ran away earlier."

"That's a pity. I really would have liked to celebrate our first big victory with an enjoyable meal."

"Maybe some other time," Jasmine said. She would have liked to go to dinner with him too, but she needed to catch up with Luffy. She also wanted to talk through the case with him and try to figure out whether Brandy really was guilty.

"Yeah. We should have plenty of chances with you back in town, I guess."

Their goodbyes were more awkward than Jasmine expected, and she thought about going to the restaurant with him just to clear up whatever the strange tension was. He was walking away before she could change her mind though, and it left her feeling strangely alone.

"You picked me over Brandon," Luffy huffed from where he was sitting on the ground.

"I guess, but that was mostly because I was mad at you. Where did you run off to, and why didn't you tell me? I was so worried about you."

"I wanted to help with the case. You were busy with Brandon, and you weren't listening to me."

"I always listen to you!" Jasmine exclaimed, a little too loudly. She got a few strange looks from people walking by, and she hurried to get out her phone and put it to her ear. She turned towards the gates and started walking home before she repeated herself. "I promise you, I pay attention when you talk. I just can't always have a full conversation, because there are many people around."

"Or just Brandon."

"Or just Brandon," Jasmine said with a sigh. "I know it sucks sometimes, but you know what kind of pressure it is for me to have to deal with these weird powers and with a normal life."

"I know how hard it is. I've been with you for every step of the way. I'm the only one who even knows about your powers."

"Yeah, so you get that side of things, and Brandon gets the other side of things. It's really hard to have conversations with both of you at once. And even if you were right, that wouldn't give you the right to run off like that. We're a team, and that means that you need to tell me where you're going."

"You weren't treating me much like a teammate earlier today. I kept telling you I thought it was Brandy Witz, and you kept ignoring me."

"Wait—you know something that points to Brandy? I was completely lost on why Lustbader was taking her in."

"I was trying to tell you about it all day," Luffy said, and he explained everything he had overheard, both on Brandy's phone call and what he had overheard from the workers. He even told her about the smell of blood coming from somewhere beneath the trailer and the scuff on the trailer wall, even if they didn't really point to Brandy.

"Huh..." Jasmine mused. They had made it back to the offices, and Jasmine struggled with the key as she tried to unlock the door. "Are you sure it was like the scuff from a sneaker?"

"Pretty sure. It smelled like rubber."

"Huh..." Jasmine repeated. She tossed her keys down on the table, but did not take off her coat just yet. It was still too cold in the building to be comfortable without it. "I guess it could be from a long time ago, but I don't see how it wouldn't be connected."

"That's what I thought too."

Jasmine grabbed her notebook and turned to a fresh page so she could sketch out her ideas. "Okay, so the only way that mark gets there is if someone puts their foot up on the side of the trailer. If you put that together with the footprints you think you saw, it's almost like someone was trying to climb onto the trailer, and then jumped down."

"That makes sense."

"Right. But why?"

She wished she had gotten to do the walkthrough with Annette to see what was out of place, but there was no point dwelling on that now.

"Maybe they were trying to get in through the window?"

"The window was too small for a person to get through. We thought that at first when we found it broken, but there's no way a human could have gotten through there."

"Then it would have to be something on the roof. Did you see anything on the roof while you were there?"

"No. I didn't even think to look."

Jasmine set her pencil down, ready to leave it at that, but her mind seemed to conjure the images of spies coming in through the roof of a building in bad heist movies. It wasn't the most practical thing in the world, but it gave her an idea. "What if the trailer had a sunroof? One of those little hatches you can open to get fresh air if it's a nice day? A lot of trailers have them, and if they take these to every carnival, I would think they might want one."

"So then the killer could have gotten in through the roof."

"Or even just dropped the body," Jasmine said, her eyes lighting up at the revelation. "This is big—we might just have figured out how the body got where it was found."

"Yeah. But the case is over. Lustbader arrested Brandy, and we don't have any reason to think that it wasn't her."

"Right..." Jasmine looked down at her sketch. "But if this is how the killer got in, then we do have some evidence to say that it wasn't Brandy. I haven't spent a lot of time around her, but she wasn't a young woman. I don't know if she could have climbed onto the roof of the trailer, even if she kicked out the window and used the frame as support."

Jasmine's eyes lit up again as she realized the origin of the bit of ice they had found on the ground. If someone wearing boots had kicked out the frame, it would make perfect sense for the impact to dislodge a bit of ice from the boot itself, to be lost forever in the pile of glass at the base of the window. It made a lot more sense than someone tossing in their tools and somehow getting a chip of ice in there too.

Then again, if it had been Georgia who committed the murder, her tools could have easily come with a chip of ice.

"I don't know. I guess it could have been her. Do you think

Lustbader would let me talk to her a bit about it?"

"I don't know. He may not have a choice anymore. Now that you've started your own firm, he may have to keep certain things private from you."

He was probably right, and Jasmine didn't really think she would feel better after a single conversation with the woman who was being taken to jail. If she was going to do this the right way, she was going to need some kind of hard evidence, and she wasn't going to get it now that she wasn't officially investigating the case. She probably couldn't even go backstage anymore, let alone into the trailer where the murder had taken place.

She needed to drop it, she realized. for the first time in her life, following the case through to the end may not be the most rational choice. If she could trust Lustbader, she could take her money and whatever prestige came from already having worked on a case, and move on.

"Okay. I guess I should probably start putting together a new ad, now that we have some experience. We should probably find a way to incorporate that."

"Right. That would be a good way to get us on the map."

"Good," Jasmine said, though she was mostly just trying to convince herself. She went upstairs to bed and lay down. Luffy took the space next to her, and between Luffy and the blankets, the cold in the room was almost bearable. She could move on from this, Jasmine tried to convince herself. She didn't need to be the one to solve the crime every time. She repeated these things to herself as she went to sleep, hoping it would make them true.

CHAPTER 7

When Jasmine woke up, she found herself almost disappointed at the lack of a vision during the night.

"No," she repeated to herself. "This is good. No more visions means that the police might solve the case. Lustbader might have found the person responsible for the murder. He might have found the killer."

"The visions are inconvenient too," Luffy reminded her as he walked past her to get to his food bowl. "You don't really want more of them, do you? You never even told me about the last one, so I'm guessing it wasn't very important."

"It was kind of important," Jasmine said, and she explained everything she could about the vision to him. She had warmed up in the night, so it was a lot easier to talk about the cold without feeling threatened or otherwise unsafe. It bothered her that the vision hadn't come true, and she realized it might have been a big part of why she was so skeptical about Brandy being the actual killer. Her visions had never failed to come true before, and she just didn't see how this one could come true if Brandy was safely put away in jail.

"That sounds scary. Was I there?"

"No. Not that I saw. I don't know where you would have gone, but you weren't there."

"So you can just stick with me, and you'll be fine."

Jasmine didn't believe it would work, but she wasn't really sure what to think about the vision not coming true. It felt like more evidence pointing towards Lustbader being wrong, but it still wasn't conclusive. She needed something conclusive to convince someone else, and there would have to be an awful lot of convincing if she wanted to get back into the case in any official capacity. Jasmine tried to push aside the thoughts and enjoy a quick breakfast. When she finished eating, she sat idly at her desk, wondering what came next.

"I guess I should take the new ad to the Book Nook. Work on getting it into the paper."

"That makes sense," Luffy agreed, but he didn't seem much more convinced than Jasmine was. "And, better yet, it means we get to go outside!"

He had perked up to his normal self again, and Jasmine tried to take solace in that. She felt really guilty about not talking to him and taking him seriously before. She didn't know whether she would have done things differently with his information, but she should have listened to him all the same. Luffy was her best friend, and she felt awful about potentially excluding him.

They walked outside, and Luffy seemed happy to walk along. Jasmine found her gaze wandering to the carnival.

"You know, someone would have seen the killer standing on the trailer. It wouldn't be any better than walking through the front door—actually, it might be worse. People would remember."

"Yeah. I bet someone would have seen something. Should we go talk to them again?"

"No," Jasmine shook her head and forced herself to look away from the carnival. "I said that our theory from before can't be right. Which means we have no reason to think it isn't Brandy."

"Other than your vision."

"Other than my vision. Which isn't exactly hard evidence."

"They've never been wrong before."

"It's not like I've had one since the case ended," Jasmine said, stepping onto the street to cross to the other side. "When there's this big of a gap, it usually means the murder hasn't happened yet."

As if her statement had been tempting fate, Jasmine felt herself go a little lightheaded. She could feel all the blood rushing through her veins and she was struck with a choice she never had to make before. She could hold the vision off if she needed to—she had done it before, and she remembered how it had felt—and she was in the middle of the street, so she probably should. At the same time, she was almost desperate for the clues that the vision would guide her to, despite being officially off the case. Blackwood Cove was not a very busy place, and traffic was sparse on the road. Barring the event she got hit by a terrible stroke of luck, she would be in the clear, even if she was passed out for quite a while.

Jasmine was so torn in her indecision that she was actively using half her brainpower to fight the vision off and half to welcome it. That, as it turned out, was certainly not enough to keep the vision at bay. After all her deliberation, it hit her.

Jasmine was outside a window. Someone had covered it with cardboard and duct tape, but there was just enough of a gap near the bottom for her to peer inside. As she did so, she could make out the features of a familiar trailer, though her view was in the opposite orientation of what she was used to. Annette was in the trailer, and instinctively Jasmine questioned why she would be there. She soon remembered that before everything had gone wrong, this trailer had been the preparation area for all the figure skaters—or at least, the ones who were really old enough to be performing.

Annette was talking to someone Jasmine had never met. She was tall and thin like her, and Jasmine guessed it was Henrietta, the other skater she had yet to meet. They were both working on their hair, staring into the same mirror. Jasmine couldn't make out their exact words, but the snippets and phrases she could pick up made her realize it was just gossip. Small talk to fill the silence.

Annetta reached over to a nearby cabinet, not even looking at her hand as she made the move. When she grasped air, she seemed confused. She turned her head to look, then noticed a small bowl of hairpins in the corner. She moved the bowl to the edge of the table and went on with her beauty routine. Every so often, she would reach into the bowl like clockwork, just like she twisted her hair around her fingers.

Jasmine kept waiting for something big to happen. Perhaps someone would come in through the door and claim the two women as the next victims. Maybe one of them would start yelling at the other. Maybe Jasmine would glimpse a shadowy figure through the ajar door of the trailer. Even something small would have explained to her why she had the vision and given her a clue, but nothing came. Jasmine watched as Annette and Henrietta put the last of their pins in their hair. They were then roused not by some dramatic event within the vision, but by the simple bark of a dog.

Jasmine expected to find herself on the ground, but she was still standing perfectly upright. Luffy had moved from directly at her side to about two feet in front of her. He had his paws planted firmly on the concrete, his head up tall, and he was barking loudly at a truck that had stopped in the center of the road. Jasmine could barely make out the driver behind the wheel, an adult man whom she had never seen before. She raised a hand in a wave to thank the man for stopping for her, but he didn't seem content with that. He turned to the side, and it took Jasmine a second to realize he was getting out of the car. Her heart raced—she didn't like confrontation, and she wasn't quite sure how she would explain to a potentially angry driver why she had been standing still in the middle of the road. After such a lackluster vision and high current stakes, it made her think she should have resisted more rather than give in to the vision.

"Are you alright?" asked the man as he got out of the truck, and Jasmine relaxed a bit when she saw he did not look particularly hostile. Though it was evidently winter in Blackwood Cove, the man looked as though he lived in a state of perpetual summer—he was incredibly tan, and the ratty ponytail of his hair was visibly sun-bleached. He squinted at Jasmine as she did likewise, both mutually assessing each other.

"You should probably answer," Luffy reminded her.

Right. An answer.

"I'm fine," she said, unconvincingly.

The man squinted at her. "You're not going to collapse as soon as I drive away, are you?"

"No. I promise."

"And you are going to get off the road?"

"Yes. I'm sorry I was in the way."

"I guess it's not my business what you're doing standing in the road as long as you're not dying. While I've got you here—you wouldn't know the way to a carnival, would you? This town is not that big, and I feel like I've driven all the way across it a dozen times."

"The Winter Wonderland carnival is just down the street," Jasmine answered, now confused who the guy was. Had he come from out of town to see the carnival in action? "Why are you heading there? Looking for fun?"

"Fun of a certain kind," he said, a glimmer in his eye. He reached into one pocket and pulled out a small box that could only be an engagement ring. "I've got a girl working there."

Jasmine's mind flipped through all of her options, trying to put together who he could be engaged to. A few names came up, but none seemed to make any more sense than the last. She figured getting out of this interaction relatively easily was more important than an answer to a trivial question, and so she didn't ask.

"Good luck," she said with a fleeting smile. She really wished him well—there were few things sadder than a failed proposal.

"Thank you. I might need it."

He got back in his car and Jasmine watched him drive away, headed in the correct direction. Once he was gone, she started walking again.

"Who do you think he was proposing to?"

"Probably no one we know. Hopefully, it goes well for him."

For a moment, the man and his potential fiancé distracted Jasmine, and it was enough to make her forget the significance of having a vision. When it came back to her, she stopped in her tracks.

"The case isn't over. We need to get back to the carnival and find out what's going on."

"Will they let us back in? You aren't working for them

anymore."

"I'll tell him there's been a mistake. We need to figure out what's going on and who the actual killer is. That needs to be our top priority."

She turned on her heel and started back towards the carnival at a furtive pace with renewed vigor. Luffy had to walk fast to keep up with her.

"What's the plan? Are we going to talk to Annette since she was in your vision?"

"I want to talk to Henrietta. She was there too, and we don't really know anything about her."

"That's a good point."

At the gate, a member of staff asked Jasmine for her ticket. She tried to get away with the ticket stub from the day before or the promise that Peter knew who she was, but it was not enough for the person holding the gate. She ended up grabbing just enough stray change out of the bottom of her purse to cover the entrance fee, making a mental note to cash the check from Peter as soon as she could.

She was familiar with the carnival, and she walked towards the ice rink. There was a show going on, so she couldn't walk up to the ice and talk to the skaters—in fact, the show was full, so she couldn't get anywhere close. She stood awkwardly outside the theater with Luffy, grateful that she had prepared for the snowy ground and worn boots.

"Maybe we should try to get backstage?" she suggested, looking down at Luffy. "We could talk to the workers you overheard, see what they have to say on the matter."

"What who has to say on what matter?"

Jasmine glanced towards the voice and was surprised to see Paul. He glided across the ice to get closer to her, petting Luffy a few times when he stopped in his chair.

"Oh... I was just going to talk to a few of their employees about their take on the case."

"Isn't the case over?"

"Yes. But I like to be thorough, make sure we've found all the evidence that we can and checked out every viable lead."

"That's cool. I applaud that, but Peter probably won't. He's been trying to erase any sign that anything happened around here. It's kind of a point of expertise for him."

"Expertise. At making problems disappear?"

"When it comes to the carnival, yeah. This place isn't as squeaky clean as it appears, but Peter will never let that show."

"It's not squeaky clean?" Jasmine asked. Not only might criminal enterprises lead to motive for murder, Peter's ability to cover them up might mean he could do the same with a murder, or at least be willing to try it. "What kind of stuff was he trying to cover up?"

"Well, I bet you haven't heard about my accident."

"I.." jasmine stammered. She knew it was rude to ask him about the chair, but now that he had brought it up, she wasn't quite sure how to handle it. "You're right, I haven't heard."

"Well, I used to have Mark's job. A few years ago, I was trying to pull off a trick that involved skating on this really thin ledge above some guests. I'd done it before and I was pretty good, so they didn't really have any reason to think I would fall. I don't think it's really their fault, but it was a little warm one day and it melted the ice more in one place than another. I slipped, fell, and it's been the chair ever since."

Paul told the story with hardly any emotion, let alone passion. It was as if he was explaining a business deal that had gone wrong, rather than something which had clearly and profoundly impacted his life.

"Peter covered that up?" Jasmine asked. She wondered if that was legal, and more importantly, if it was moral.

"He did just about what he did with Mark's death. He got the right people involved, had them handle it as quietly as possible, and did everything just right so the media wouldn't have anything to sink their teeth into. Eventually, people stopped asking. Somehow it avoided becoming a media sensation."

"That's how he keeps the underage skaters quiet too."

"You know about that? I guess you did interview quite a few of the people around here. You're right, though. He uses this special charming compliance to make it seem like he's not doing wrong— every time you ask him a question, he responds with something to make you feel better. It makes it hard to write a truthful story criticizing how Peter or the carnival handle incidents, which kills the drama."

"I still think it would be a pretty big story for a stunt-man to fall in the middle of a stunt."

"Not really. Peter didn't tell anyone how badly I was injured, or if I had been injured at all. He treated the whole thing so casually that even the most intrepid reporters grew bored pretty quick."

"Wow. That's really terrible—I'm sorry."

"Doesn't bother me," Paul said with a shrug. "It was probably the right move for the carnival, which means that I still have a job. I'd honestly prefer radio silence on the matter, just like the skaters would prefer not to be turned in. We're happy here, and Peter's working to make sure that things don't change."

Jasmine found Paul's description of Peter rather sinister. He was painting the man as a puppet-master who pulled strings behind the scenes to keep secrets from the public. Even if the overall outcome worked out, his manipulations of public opinion was anything but desirable. Secrets were to be kept hidden, and people lashed out when they were threatened to be revealed—sometimes even in deadly ways.

"Were you close with Mark?" Jasmine asked. Her attention had been diverted entirely away from the ice now as she considered this new angle to the case.

"Not particularly. I showed him the ropes when he first took my job, but the man was a professional skater—he didn't need much guidance."

"Did you tell him about how you were injured?"

"Peter discontinued the trick after I fell, so it wasn't a safety issue he needed to know about. I'm sure it got around to him though—Peter kept it pretty quiet outside of the carnival, but I was still recovering at the time and pretty much everyone around here knew what it was from."

It seemed far-fetched to think Mark could have been ignorant of the circumstances. Her first thought had been about Mark finding out about Peter's cover-up. Fear for his own life and a desire for the spotlight could have enticed Mark to share it with the public in some juicy tell-all. If Peter was determined to keep him quiet, murder might have been the next step to make sure that happened. Someone would have had to entice Mark to share the secret, and Jasmine wondered what could have possibly motivated the man.

"Can you think of anything else that Peter was trying to hide?"

"Do you want years' worth of tiny slights or just the highlights? We're a traveling carnival—we had our fair share of problems, and Peter's covered them all up. I could run you through everything we've ever done wrong, but I think it would be a waste of both of our time."

Jasmine thought about asking him to tell her anyway, but he was probably right. A small health code violation with the way they had set up a food tent two years ago was probably not going to have too much of an effect on the case.

"What about big things? I mean, it paralyzed you... have there been any other big events like that?"

"Not really. No one's been hurt. We had to replace a trailer a while back after one of Georgia's liquid nitrogen tanks exploded, though."

"It exploded?"

"We were surprised too. It was just after we had hired this supposed specialist, and there was something about the pressure being all wrong."

"It must have been difficult to get the new trailer set up," Jasmine said, thinking back to just how specialized the ice trailer had been. "I mean, the costs to replace the cooling gear alone must have been substantial."

"The cooling gear? Oh—no, it wasn't the ice management trailer that got damaged. It was the trailer where the skaters get ready. For certain shows, they have tiaras and jewelry that are made of ice. Georgia drags the tank into their trailer and freezes them there, right before they go on. I think she would rather do it in her workshop, but some pieces have to be specifically tailored to the skaters."

"Wait, I think I've seen the liquid nitrogen tanks," Luffy said, and he described to Jasmine what he had seen behind Georgia's trailer. The tanks he described were bigger than Jasmine had imagined.

"Wait, so Georgia can just carry a big tank like that into another trailer and no one bats an eye?"

"It's part of her job," Paul agreed, as if it was the most natural thing in the world.

Jasmine remembered the ice-cold room of her vision and the strange suit the person locking her in there had been wearing. It had looked an awful lot like Georgia's outfit that she had been wearing to handle the ice, and she could easily imagine one of the liquid nitrogen tanks strapped to the back. Georgia could have transported Mark's body in an empty liquid nitrogen tank, and the rest of the suit would have protected her from leaving behind any evidence while she was at the crime scene. No one would have been surprised by her showing up there in her suit and a tank, as Paul had verified.

"Thank you. I think there are some people I want to go talk to."

She started walking away, but Paul stopped her.

"You cannot get backstage by yourself."

"I think I'll be fine. I know where it is, and I've gone there on my own before."

"You went there on your own while you had permission to be there. Everyone knows the investigation is over. You can't go by yourself."

It took Jasmine a moment to realize he was trying to convince her he needed to be there too. She didn't know whether he was really trying to get her past some extra security that they had in place, or if he had some kind of ulterior motive. Either way, she wasn't sure what difference him being there could make. At the very least, she could let him get her through security, and then she could go off with Luffy to ask a few questions.

"Will you take us backstage? I really want to make sure we've got the right person behind bars."

"Of course I will," Paul said with a smile. He pushed his chair along, and Jasmine and Luffy followed him.

"Are you going to ignore me for him now?" Luffy asked as they went.

"Hey, Paul," Jasmine said, getting her phone out of her bag and putting one earbud in her ear. "Would it be okay if I talked to my partner as we went? I want to keep him up to date with everything that's going on."

"Sure…" Paul said, sounding a little confused. "Aren't we just making sure everything is in line? I would have thought you'd talk to a partner more during the actual investigation than this obligatory review."

"He likes to hear about everything. Don't worry, he shouldn't really impede conversation. I'll make a few comments to him, but other than that it shouldn't be too intrusive."

"Okay," Paul said with a shrug. "I guess that's fine. The earbuds make you look less like a cop too, so Peter will like that."

"That was really smart," Luffy said. "Now we can talk all we want."

"Right," Jasmine said, and though it wasn't quite clear who she was responding to. Neither minded the confusion much at all.

Paul took them through the same gate as they had gone through before. He paused on the other side to switch back to his wheels, then turned around to look at Jasmine.

"You seemed to have someone in mind to talk to. I can help you find them and act as your all-access path to the backstage area. So, where are we heading?"

Jasmine was most suspicious of Georgia, but she had already spoken to her once. She doubted she would get any kind of admission to anything just by talking to her again, which meant it was probably better to check out another source. Her first thought was to walk around and ask if anyone had seen her entering the trailer. She hesitated, trying to think of whom to talk to, and was caught rather off guard when she saw a familiar face.

"You're zombie girl," said the guy who had nearly run her over earlier. He looked at her quizzically, as if he was seeing a ghost or an alien. "What are you doing here? I thought you were headed the other way?"

"You know this dude?" Paul asked.

"Not really."

"We ran into each other earlier," he said. "Now I'm sorry to ask you guys this, but is there any chance you could get out of the way? I think I want a bit of space for this."

Jasmine knew he had to be talking about the ring he had been carrying when they first spoke. She didn't see a woman around, and the only man around was Paul, who clearly hadn't known who this guy was. She had no idea who the guy was going to propose to, or where he would want space around for the major event. She stepped directly backwards in the vague hope that it would be away from the area he was trying to claim, and he seemed satisfied.

Jasmine watched carefully as he moved to the side, and it surprised her when he turned not to a person, but to a door. It was the only closed door on any trailer backstage, which made it instantly memorable and recognizable. The man knocked on the door firmly a few times. Jasmine waited for him to get a response, before she remembered how things had gone when she had tried the same tactic. She nudged Paul's shoulder. If this was going where she expected it to go, she didn't want such a mundane difficulty to break up the flow of the event.

"Text Georgia. Get her to come outside."

Paul pulled out his phone and did what he was told. He didn't seem to understand or know the full context of the event, but he was willing to be helpful.

A few seconds later, Georgia opened the door. She had bulky headphones around her neck and thick gloves over her hands, and she was holding the same small hatchet Jasmine had seen her use the other day.

"Who--" she started to ask, but then her eyes landed on the person in front of her. Her eyes seemed almost to light up, and she tossed the hatchet back into the cabin rather haphazardly. "What are you doing here?"

"I had to see you," the man said, and in the next breath, he dropped to one knee. Georgia gasped, her hand going to her mouth like she was in a movie. She looked genuinely like she was about to cry, and Jasmine quickly whipped out her phone. There was a part of her that thought Georgia was a killer, but a much larger part of her thought she would appreciate photos of her engagement someday.

"Are you...?" Georgia left the question in the air to be replaced by another, more important one.

"Yes, Georgia—I'm asking you to make me the happiest man in the world and agree to marry me."

Georgia laughed, and she jumped down out of the trailer, running into the man's arms.

"Yes," she answered, and then repeated herself again as they seemed to meld together. "Yes, Danny, I will marry you."

Danny? Jasmine could not immediately place the name, but she felt sure she had heard it somewhere before.

"Like Brandy's Danny," Luffy said, getting to the answer faster than Jasmine.

"Yes. That's where I'd heard that before."

She realized she was still taking a video, and her voice was going to be picked up on the recording. She didn't think that Georgia would want to hear her stray comments in the video, so she was careful to be quiet until the couple pulled apart and it seemed like a good time to stop the video. She could get Georgia's number if she interviewed her again later, and send her the video, but for now it only seemed fair to leave them to their love story.

She was ready to interview the other employees, but they too seemed caught up. As Jasmine walked away from the proposal, there were lots of people moving towards it. Some of them seemed excited, others just interested in seeing what was going on. Jasmine thought she caught a few people gossiping about the supposed affair between Georgia and Mark, but they were all past Jasmine before she could identify the people talking.

She expected her all-access pass to the backstage would follow her out of the crowd, but Paul stayed where he was. She checked to see if he needed help to escape the newly formed crowd, but he didn't seem stuck. In fact, he was moving towards the happy couple, and Jasmine remembered Georgia's earlier comment about how it was always good to see him around. They were friends, so naturally he would want to talk to her about the engagement. It seemed odd that Paul hadn't seemed to recognize Danny at all—he seemed close to both Brandy and Georgia..

"Where are we headed next?" Luffy asked once they were clear of the rush of workers.

"Well, I was going to talk to everyone. But that will not happen now. I was thinking maybe we go straight to Peter. Some of those things Paul said made it seem like he might not care about anything other than keeping the carnival afloat. I can picture him going to drastic lengths to make that happen."

"Doesn't Peter not want us here? Won't he just kick you out?"

"We won't frame it like we're investigating. We'll just say we want to talk to him."

A quick consult with one of the outermost employees of the crowd pointed Jasmine to the correct trailer. The door was as wide open as the others, and at first she wondered if Peter really just left his personal trailer open to everyone. She awkwardly knocked on the outside of the trailer—she didn't want to go inside without permission, as it felt like crossing a barrier.

"You know you can come in!" Peter's voice radiated from inside. He couldn't know that it was Jasmine, so the instructions weren't really meant for her only. Still, she took it as an invitation which applied to her and stepped into the trailer.

Well before she saw Peter, she saw Diana. The girl was sitting in a folding chair against the nearest counter, holding a pencil and working on some paper Jasmine couldn't see from where she stood.

"Hi Diana," Jasmine greeted, prompting the girl to look up.

"Hey. What are you doing here? I thought that old dude beat you to solving the case."

"Lustbader isn't that old."

"He's old enough that you knew who I was talking about," Diana said, and she went back to her paper.

Jasmine would have been more than happy to leave the interaction there, but when she looked around the trailer, she didn't see Peter. It wasn't a huge trailer, and she had clearly heard him letting her in, so she knew he had to be there.

"Where's your dad?"

"He's in his office. What do you want from him?"

"I just wanted to talk to him a bit."

"I saw how much he paid you. You didn't even solve the case. You really shouldn't be begging for more."

"That's not why I'm here."

"Yes, it is. It may not be in the form of another check, but everything has to do with money."

Jasmine wasn't sure how she felt about a thirteen-year-old giving her cynical readings of the world, and she thought it best to change the subject.

"Can I just go into your dad's office, or should I wait out here?"

"Wait out here. He gets really mad when anyone goes into his office."

Jasmine wasn't sure how that would fit together with the open entry to his trailer, but there was a closed door blocking off part of the interior. She stayed awkwardly where she was, waiting for Peter to come out of his office. Diana did not seem keen to start up a conversation to fill the silence, so Jasmine took matters into her own hands.

"So what are you working on, Diana? Is it school work?"

"I don't go to school."

"I meant like home school work."

"I don't really do that either. My dad makes me do worksheets and read books in the mornings when the other girls are skating, but it's not like I have a teacher."

"Well, are you working on your worksheets and books?" Jasmine asked, checking the clock. It was still morning, so it would make sense if Diana was doing her work.

"No."

Jasmine was getting frustrated with the conversation, and she stepped forward a couple of steps in order to see what Diana was working on. It wasn't a worksheet or anything academical, but a drawing.

It was a fairly accurate sketch, and it impressed Jasmine how Diana was using light to convey the image. She was, however, more concerned. The focal point of the picture was a dead body, slumped against a nondescript wall with a thick jacket pulled back just far enough to reveal small, colorless gashes in the wrists.

"Is that Mark?" Jasmine asked as Diana covered up the sketch.

"It's my personal art," Diana said, her voice rising both in pitch and volume as she defended herself. "You don't have any right to look at it."

"What's all the commotion?" Peter asked, pushing his office door open. Jasmine worried that the commotion they had been making counted as disturbing him in his office, and that she was now going to face his fury. Peter didn't look mad, but when he saw Jasmine, he seemed confused.

"Jasmine," he said, looked down at Luffy with a mix of fear and concern that he admirably attempted to hide. "I'm surprised to see you here."

"Sorry, sir," Jasmine said, though she had not been accused of anything yet. "I just wanted to ask you a few questions about the carnival."

"You could have come in," he said, then looked around her at Diana. "Are you still hanging out in here? What happened to those friends of yours? A couple of days ago, you were inseparable."

"We're still friends. They just only ever want to skate, and sometimes I enjoy doing things other than being on the ice."

Peter sighed. "Sorry about her. She's been tense ever since everything happened with Mark. We can leave her here and step into my office if you want."

"Okay," Jasmine said, but she was worried about Diana now. She wasn't hanging out with her friends and preferred drawing pictures of a dead body. It sort of seemed like the murder was taking a harder toll on the teenager than she was letting on.

"I can stay with Diana," Luffy said, apparently thinking along the same lines. "You should probably focus on Peter anyway, and she looks like she could use some company."

Jasmine nodded. It was a good idea. Jasmine didn't know much about helping people deal with death, but she didn't think having a dog as cute as Luffy around could do anything other than help.

"I think Luffy will wait out here, if that's okay. He doesn't need to be there for our chat."

"Okay," Peter said with a casual shrug. He didn't do a great job of hiding the look of relief on his face, so Jasmine could still tell he was happy about the news. She wondered how he was so good at hiding things on a professional level when he didn't seem to have much of a poker face at all.

Peter's so-called office was at the spot in the trailer where the bedroom was meant to be. It was a small space with a cheap and thin folding door to separate it from the outside.

"What was it you wanted to talk about? I was pretty sure I'd already done my interview for the local paper."

"I'm not with the local paper. I'm a private investigator, remember? You hired me."

"I knew that. But everyone here at the carnival wears many hats, and I'm sure it's the same in a town as small as this. Your mayor probably works in the local coffee shop. For someone as young as you, being a small-time private investigator would go hand in hand with being a field journalist."

"I'm not a journalist," Jasmine said, though she had gone to school for writing and likely could have worked at the local paper if she wanted to. "I'm just asking a few questions as myself. The private investigator."

"Alright," Peter said with a bit of a chuckle. "Is this something that I need to be concerned about?"

"No, of course not. Sheriff Lustbader already arrested someone for the recent murder. If that's everything the carnival has to hide, you should have nothing to worry about."

"I see," Peter replied, looking skeptical. He closed a folder that had been open on his desktop and looked up at Jasmine. "Well, if we're not chatting about the murder, what can I help you with?"

"I heard a few things during my investigation. Apparently you have a habit—and a skill—for making it look like there's nothing that goes wrong with the carnival."

"I'm sure they're going on about those few cases where the media tried to turn against us. I have a knack for quieting anything false that they may try to print, but I would never impede a truthful review."

"I'm not saying you're lying to anyone. I've just heard that you're quite good at making the truth sound as good as it can."

"Of course I am. I work at a carnival. We sell the fantastical as part of our job description."

"Well, is there anything that has involved the carnival which you have a special interest in keeping the public separate from?" Jasmine pressed on, hoping a slightly different angle of questioning might be a little more helpful. She was determined to pry a direct answer out of Peter, even if that took some work.

"I'm sorry, Jasmine. My answer would be different if you were still working on the case, but now that the carnival is in the clear again, I really don't think that this is information you need."

Jasmine wanted to argue that she was still working on the case, but Peter was looking annoyed with her. She figured that if she did not change topics, she would quickly overstay her welcome.

"Right. Sorry. Can I just ask who has access to Georgia's little ice chamber?"

"Whoever she lets in. I don't regulate it personally. We only keep it locked to keep people from leaving the door open after checking out the sculptures."

"Is she the only one with a key?"

"Yes. Well, maybe not. I think I have one somewhere, but I'd be hard pressed to find it for you. Do you need it in there?"

"No. I'm trying to cover all of my bases."

"Why exactly are you here?" Peter asked. His tone was light, as if he didn't really care about the answer, but the look on his face gave away that he did.

"Just to talk," Jasmine said, trying to hold on to that same light tone.

"That's sweet, but I'm busy," Peter said, standing. "It's nice of you to stop by, but maybe you can email me if you have any more questions."

Jasmine allowed herself to be gently banished from the room, though she was growing ever more suspicious by the minute. Luffy was waiting for her outside, and Diana was still working on the same drawing as before. She seemed to focus on it rather intently.

"She barely even looked at me," Luffy said. "I'm really worried about her."

"Are you doing okay, Diana?" Jasmine asked as Peter nudged her closer to the door.

"I'm good," Diana replied without looking up.

"Let me know if you need anything, or want to talk. I've seen a lot of messed up situations. I might be able to help."

"Diana is fine," Peter said, and he was moving towards the door so Jasmine had no choice but to do the same. "I think it's time for you to go back into the carnival. I can offer you a free ticket for any of our rides or attractions. I know you and your friend were here together the other day, so if you need a second ticket for him, I might even make that happen. What rides did you like again? I seem to have forgotten."

"We like the ice slides," Jasmine said, surprised by the question. She needed to go talk to Georgia, not head back to the carnival. Besides, Brandon wasn't even there with her. Before she could say anything further, Peter was reaching into a fanny pack Jasmine hadn't even noticed he was wearing. He handed Jasmine two small tickets, which reminded her of the ones used on the rides.

"Have a good time. That's what the carnival is for."

Jasmine walked away, but she stopped after only a few feet to talk to Luffy.

"So Diana just ignored you?"

"Yes. I even tried begging, but she wouldn't give me any attention. She was so focused on her drawing."

"She was drawing a dead body. It was Mark's body."

"She saw it when she visited the crime scene."

"Yeah. And she's young, so that might have been more than she was ready to handle. I'm worried about her."

"I am too."

They stood there, working together to think of some way they could help the girl. When nothing came to mind, Jasmine shook her head and walked again.

"Where are we going?"

"Back into the carnival. I don't want to interrupt Georgia with an interview right after she got engaged, and Peter will be keeping an eye out for us now. We should lie low for an hour. Maybe even use the ticket he gave us."

"You want to take a break?"

"I don't see a path to getting any additional information from a reliable source anytime soon. A break won't kill us. We can look through things, try to put the pieces together. I'm still trying to figure out the evidence you found behind the trailer—I'm really starting to think that the killer came in through the front door, wearing a full suit like Georgia's. That really raises the question of why anyone would be back there behind the trailer to begin with."

"Shouldn't we figure that out by talking to people?"

"We will. Just not yet."

They walked back through the gate that led them to the carnival. As Jasmine noticed the employee watching the gate, it reminded her they may not get back in without help from Paul or someone else. She stood by her decision to head back out to the carnival and headed first for the slides she had just gotten a ticket to.

Jasmine didn't really need to go to the ticket counter, but she wanted to make sure that the free ticket Peter had given her would be valid. She had just been with Paul backstage, so it was not a huge surprise when he was not behind the counter. Instead, the bored teenager from a few days before was sitting behind the table, leaning on his arm.

"One ticket?" Rick asked, his stare blank as he looked up at

Jasmine.

"I wanted to see if these were valid," Jasmine said, pushing her free tickets across the table. "I got them from Peter, but I thought the normal ones looked a little different."

"They do," Rick said. "Take them up anyway. We all kind of have to listen to what Peter says."

Jasmine was about to walk away, but she remembered how her interview with Rick had been interrupted earlier that day, and she turned to look at him.

"Hey. Have you been in Georgia's trailer recently? The one with all the ice?"

"I help her haul the ice sculptures," Rick said with a shrug. He glanced over at his phone that was sitting face down on the edge of the table. I'm there pretty much all the time."

"You wouldn't have picked up any of her little wasted ice chips, would you?"

"I always pick up a few." Rick leaned to the side and looked out at the line that was snaking back and forth behind Jasmine. "You should probably move. There are people waiting."

"Why do you take them?" Jasmine asked. Ever since she had decided that someone must have worn Georgia's suit, she hadn't been thinking much about where the ice chip would have come from. It could have gotten caught up in her clothes or stuck to her shoes or even connected to the edge of the liquid nitrogen tank. It seemed mostly inconsequential now, but Rick's admission to taking the ice played into Georgia's depiction of him as a delinquent.

"I used to think I could do Georgia's thing. With the ice sculptures. I mostly gave up, but snatching the scraps kind of turned into a habit."

"Huh," Jasmine said. She hadn't pegged Rick as the sort to have a lot of ambition. "So you would know a bit about Georgia's equipment."

"I know how most of it works, but I can't put together a good sculpture to save my life. That's why I work here, but it's starting to look like I don't even have the skills to keep the line moving forward."

He said the last part with a pointed glare at Jasmine, clearly trying to send her a message about her holding up the line. There were people waiting, and Jasmine knew she was probably impeding the perfect holiday experience the carnival was promising. She wondered if Rick would talk to her again later.

"I'm going. I'd love to hear a little more about your hobby, though. Maybe I could help you get through to Georgia. She's probably in a good mood after her engagement. Maybe she'll be more willing to take on an apprentice of sorts."

"She got engaged?" Rick asked, his eyes widening in the first genuine show of emotion since Jasmine had met him. "To who, that Danny guy?"

"I think so. He doesn't work at the carnival, I don't think."

"That's probably Danny then," Rick concluded, and he looked so happy that it confused Jasmine. She wouldn't have guessed Georgia and Rick were that close, and he would care much to hear about her engagement. "Did he say anything about what their plans for the future looked like?"

"I don't know. I didn't hang around much after the actual proposal."

"There's no way Danny will hang around the carnival. We'll have to get someone to replace Georgia, I'm sure of it."

"Is that a good thing?"

"They might teach me. I could get back into sculpting. Maybe I could even pick up enough to make a proper job out of it."

There was a real sparkle in his eyes, showcasing the passion Jasmine wouldn't have ever expected to see. He seemed to notice it too, and when he realized Jasmine was still looking at him, his shoulders slumped a bit.

"It's not like it means the world to me or anything. But there aren't a lot of jobs out there that wouldn't beat standing out here on my own, pretending I enjoy selling people tickets for a ride I never get to go on."

"Right," Jasmine said, indulging his desire to project an image of being indifferent. She understood the urge more than she would admit. "I understand, but I didn't know Georgia wasn't teaching you."

"No. She did when I was a kid. When I was ten or eleven, she gave me a key to the stupid trailer. It wasn't a big deal at all, but I was young and I wanted it to be, so she did. Everyone knew."

"So you have a key to the trailer?" Jasmine asked, realizing that he would have been one of the few people with access to the suits and the know-how necessary to open one of the big vats meant for liquid nitrogen.

"Not anymore. About a year after I got it, I lost it. Georgia will tell the story a little differently, but I swear I just misplaced the thing. The next day, I went to her trailer, expecting to be shown an alternative way to shear off the ice without cracking the foundation. But she's in a rage. She had this really delicate necklace from some former flame, and someone had taken it. She said I was the only one who could have done so because I was the only one with another key to the trailer."

"What about Peter? Doesn't he keep his own key?"

"Yeah. No one ever really counts him with things like that. I mean, the guy's pretty rich. Even I can see pretty easily why he wouldn't be considered as an actual suspect for something like that."

"So she stopped teaching you over a suspicion?" Jasmine asked. She understood Georgia's earlier comment about him more now, having heard his side of the story. She didn't know if she believed Rick about his loss of the key, but it seemed odd that Peter had been disregarded as a suspect.

"She's called me a thief ever since."

"You are a thief," said the man behind Jasmine. He must have been drawn in from out of town, because Jasmine didn't recognize him. "You're stealing everyone's time. We paid to be at this carnival young man, and you're wasting our time and money with your pointless personal conversations. I have half a mind to report you to whoever your manager is."

Rick glanced back at Jasmine, and this time it was a distinct look. Apparently, being willing to hear his side of the story had garnered her enough goodwill, even if it wasn't enough to buy her interview a little more time.

"Thanks for the chat. I'm going to go test out these tickets that Peter gave me."

"Probably a good idea. I get off my shift in a couple of hours if you need something else."

Jasmine thanked him again and walked away. Luffy trotted along beside her.

"He's actually not so bad. Who is he again?"

"I don't know. I kind of thought that he was just a summer worker or something, but from the way he was talking about being here as a kid, he might belong to one of the performers."

"Which one?"

"I don't have the faintest clue. Maybe we should ask about it in our next interview."

Luffy seemed to agree, and Jasmine handed off her ticket to the man who took it. Luffy stayed behind, and Jasmine headed towards the stairs. The line was long, and she would have to wait a good while if she wanted to ride. She had waited in a similar sized line with Brandon, but it had seemed to pass a lot faster with him around, even if he was chatting with her about random things.

She remembered their debate about the ramps being hollow versus solid, and she looked for evidence to prove her point. Somewhere, just under the staircase leading to the top, she thought she made out a bit of a seam, and she tilted her head far enough over the edge to make herself look silly. It was then she noticed what seemed to be a seam of sorts starting to shift.

Jasmine practically ran down the stairs when she saw the gap widening, and she was at the bottom in time to see a familiar face leaving through what appeared to be a door.

"Annette?" she asked, rather surprised to see the skater. She was alone, and in ordinary clothes.

"Oh, hey Jasmine. Didn't they solve that case you were so worried about?"

"Yeah. Did you just come from inside the ramp?"

"Oh, yeah. They couldn't possibly make this thing solid all the way through, so they left a sizeable gap in the middle. Henrietta and I use it as a break room, just to wind down in between shows."

"So it's hollow?" Jasmine reiterated. It was pretty clear by this point it was hollow, but she needed to make sure, for the sake of argument.

"Yeah, completely. It's like a room in there. Do you want to see?"

"I'm good," Jasmine answered. She was curious about the interior, but there were far more important things she could ask Annette about. "If you have a minute, do you think we could go do that walkthrough of the trailer you agreed to a while back?"

"You still want to do that? Isn't the case over?"

"Yes," Jasmine said, reminding herself she didn't have the authority that she had gotten used to. She felt as though they had pushed her back to square one with her credibility—a kid trying to gather clues, much in the same way that she had been during her first ever case. "I like to tie up all the loose ends before I give up on a case."

"So it's basically just procedure?"

"Yes," Jasmine said, hoping it was the answer that would get her the result she wanted. "Just procedure."

"Okay. I've got about ten minutes, and I don't think it will take longer than that. We don't really have time to stop though, so you'll have to ditch the ride. You were in line a second ago, right?"

"Yeah. It's not a big deal, though. I would really much rather see what's going on in the trailer."

"Kind of a weird choice, but up to you."

They had already walked away before Jasmine remembered Luffy wasn't with them.

"Could I just go grab my dog?"

"We don't really have the time," Annette said, tilting her head. Jasmine looked back towards Luffy, then nodded and kept following. She didn't mean to leave him behind, but it would only be for a couple of minutes. With the line for the ice slide as long as it was, this version of events would probably end up being a lot faster.

The silence between them as they walked was awkward, and

Jasmine attempted to break it and get a bit of information at the same time.

"So there's a teenager named Rick who works around here," Jasmine said, assuming the crew was small enough that Annette would know who she was talking about. "Do you know if he was brought up around the carnival like the girls who skate with you?"

"Pretty much. He wasn't born into it, but I doubt he remembers life off the road. He was really young back when this whole place started up."

"So he has to be someone's kid then. Do you know whose kid he is?"

"Of course. He's mine."

Jasmine nearly stopped in her tracks from sheer surprise, but she refrained herself. Annette did not seem much like a mother to her, given her young features, petite frame and the carelessness she had shown when talking about Georgia and her children. She was resentful of Georgia and Jasmine had assumed Georgia's motherhood had been wrapped up into that, but it clearly couldn't be the case if Annette was a mother too.

"I know I was young. It's not a secret."

"No, that's not it. "I wouldn't have put that together on my own."

"Few people would have. He doesn't have much of an aptitude for the ice, and I think he looks more like his father."

If Rick outdated the carnival by a few years, his father's identity wouldn't matter, but his lack of skating talent might make itself relevant.

"Rick can't skate? I assumed anyone raised in a carnival like this would be pretty good at it."

"He's okay at it. And of course, as his mother, I'm very proud of him. But he has never really taken to it in the way that some of the girls have."

Jasmine thought about bringing up the ice sculpting, but didn't bother. She was sure Annette knew all about her son's past hobby and current interest.

"Has he ever performed with you guys on stage?"

"We thought about it a couple of years back. He was almost good enough. But we've never had a man perform with us on stage, and we weren't sure he was the best place to start."

Jasmine remembered what Brandy had said about her husband and his passion for skating.

"What about Mark? He never came on the ice with you?"

"No. He did his own thing, and that was good for him. I think he got more attention from the elites for all his stunt-work than the rest of us get for what we do. Since we're just doing the same tricks over again, ours doesn't really push the sport to its limits. Mark's didn't either, but he had this deadly precision that even some of the more talented skaters were jealous of. Nothing he does is hard, but it always impresses people when they can see someone do something like that a hundred times without screwing up once."

"That's what happened to Paul, right? He just messed up once."

"That was plain bad luck. It's not actually all that dangerous."

Jasmine didn't really agree, but they were nearing the trailer now, and she didn't take the time to contradict her. The door was as wide open as always, and when they stepped inside, it was like things had frozen in time. The body was gone, but otherwise the room showed no signs of being used. The space where Mark once had been now felt huge, despite the relatively small size of the trailer. The air felt a little still, as if the trailer remembered it had at one point carried a dead body. It took Jasmine a moment to remember why she was there at all.

"Do you see anything out of place?"

"Not really," Annette answered. She looked around slowly, scanning the room for any sign of the things she should be looking for. "I mean, I come in here all the time, so I've kind of gotten used to tuning out the surroundings."

"Nothing?" Jasmine prompted. She didn't know what she was looking for anymore. She felt sure someone would have picked up any obvious traces of the murder a long time ago. Besides, the skaters could have unconsciously corrected anything that wasn't quite in place, as Annette had done in her vision. She checked the counter to see if that vision might already have come to pass and spotted the tin of hairpins near the edge where Annette had moved it to in her vision.

"The window is broken," Annette said, stating the obvious. "And we moved one of the costume racks to our little break room, just because everyone else was hanging around here."

Annette paused and looked around. Her eyes landed on the container of hair pins, and Jasmine wondered if she was going to mention that they had been out of place before. Instead, Annette reached for them and pushed them back away from the edge of the counter.

"That goes further back," Annette said casually, as if it wasn't a big deal.

Jasmine didn't know what to do with the inconsistency. She could clearly envision Annette pulling the little container back to the edge and then using it as if it had always been there. She was trying to think if she could be remembering things wrong—her visions were always hard to remember, being hazy in the same way as a dream you had barely held on to. She hadn't even thought to write it down for its insignificance, but now she was really wishing that she had.

"You think the killer moved that?"

"Probably not on purpose. I don't know. I'm mostly just trying to help."

"Right," Jasmine remarked. She knew there wasn't any basis for asking any more questions, and she wasn't even sure it was an inconsistency, so she tried to move past it.

"Is there anything else I can help with?" Annette asked. She sounded like she was just about done with helping Jasmine with the task at hand. Jasmine wished she could have gotten more information out of the walkthrough, but it didn't seem likely to happen.

"Let me know if you learn anything new."

"I will. I should probably get ready for my next show, though."

"Of course," Jasmine agreed, and she voluntarily let herself out of the trailer. She was ready to go back to see Luffy, but she noticed that Georgia's kids were kicking a ball around in the center of the backstage area. She hadn't seen them off the ice before and was surprised by how much like normal kids they looked when the sparkly uniforms and makeup were traded in for hoodies and frizzy ponytails.

"Are you two not performing today?" she asked as she walked over.

"Not today," Charlie answered. "Peter doesn't let us on the ice for a little while after something big happens."

"He thinks we're too little to handle a little extra pressure while we skate," Eve added. "He's wrong, but we have to listen to him."

Peter seemed nice, but the more Jasmine heard the way others talked about him, the less she felt he could be trusted. Keeping the kids from preforming on days after controversy felt very much like a ploy to keep the public from noticing the discrepancy while the carnival was still in the public eye. Also, the last few people Jasmine had talked to had repeated the same line about having to obey Peter, no matter the circumstance.

"Where's Diana?" Jasmine asked, looking around for the girl.

"She doesn't play with us anymore," Eve declared.

"She'll play with us," Charlie said. "We're just always playing our little kid games, and she doesn't want to play little kid games."

"She doesn't want to skate either. That's big kid stuff. Auntie Annette said so."

"Auntie Annette also said that we have to leave Diana alone," Charlie reminded her sister, then looked up at Jasmine. "I don't think Diana's been doing a very good job of dealing with the case. She brags about having seen the body, but I think she might be one of the people who can't handle that."

"I could handle it."

"No, you wouldn't. You're just a little kid. You probably would cry."

"I would not!" Eve retorted, and they fought again like how siblings always seemed to. Jasmine was really glad she didn't have to deal with any.

What she needed to deal with was whatever was going on with Diana. She knew the girl wasn't her responsibility, but she was really starting to get worried. If Diana was pulling away from whatever her interests had been, that was a bad sign. When it had only been skating she was avoiding, it might just have been a coincidence that she grew bored with the sport around the same time that Jasmine got there. If she was also pulling away from her social circle, that was a terrible sign.

She knew she wasn't likely to be welcome back in Peter's trailer so soon after he had ushered her out, but she went there anyway. Jasmine was pretty sure it would be okay for her to enter without knocking based on what they had been saying earlier, but she still knocked on the side of the trailer. It would be especially rude just to barge into a place where she really wasn't welcome.

When her knock didn't get a response, she tried a verbal approach. "Peter? Diana?"

For an awful second, Jasmine harbored the idea that they could have been the next victim of whoever had killed Mark, and she stepped into the trailer mostly to deny that horrible suspicion. The main room was empty, Diana's drawings discarded on the counter. The door to Peter's office was partially ajar, and open enough for Jasmine to see that he was not there, or at least not sitting at his desk.

"Hello?" she called out again, but there was still no response. Just to be sure that Peter wasn't lying dead on the ground in his office, she poked her head into the small chamber. When that didn't give her the angle she wanted, she stepped all the way into the room to prove to herself that Peter's body was nowhere to be found. He was likely to be very much alive and out in the world, doing his job. She had missed him, but that wasn't a tremendous deal.

She thought about waiting for him or coming back later, but neither seemed like a good option. She needed to get back to Luffy, and she had no way of knowing when Peter would be back and whether he would even be willing to listen to whatever she had to say when he eventually did. She looked around for another way to handle things, and her eyes landed on the pens he kept on his desk. She pulled out a page of her notebook and a pen of her own to leave him a note, leaning against his desk to stabilize the notebook. She didn't have a lot of expert advice about what to do with her, but she wanted Peter to be well aware of what was going on with his daughter.

Jasmine was trying to decide where to put the note when she noticed the file folder open on Peter's desk. She didn't mean to snoop, but the picture caught her eye. She was pretty sure it was Rick. He wasn't smiling, and he was a few years younger. She was curious about what Peter could be looking into the boy for, and she turned her head just enough to read the writing. It surprised her to see what looked like a resume from the boy.

She moved around the desk to get a better look. The skating skills seemed to have been exaggerated, and there was no mention of the things he had told her. It took Jasmine a minute to realize he was applying for the job that Mark had once held. It surprised her a little, but it didn't hold her interest for much longer than a few seconds.

The same could not be said for the files sticking out of a partially open desk drawer. It looked like they had been hastily shoved away, and if Jasmine had not come to that side of the desk, she never would have noticed the difference. She rationalized her decision by reminding herself she was already snooping where she shouldn't be, and it wouldn't really be any worse for her to grab the files out of the drawer and look at something interesting.

The main folder that was sticking out was blue, and when she opened it she was greeted with a stack of letters written in a messy script. Most of them were written on torn paper and filled with countless signs that the writer had not put even a bit of care into his work. Jasmine could hardly read the handwriting to make out the content of the letter, but a single glance at the bottom of the page confirmed they were from Danny. She was beginning to think she needed to talk to this Danny guy, and figure out how and why he was connected to practically everyone in the carnival.

"You shouldn't be in here."

Jasmine looked up, startled by the voice, and saw that Diana was standing in the doorway. Jasmine stood up tall, as if it would be enough to reinstate the authority she didn't have.

"Your dad said I could look at a few things in here."

"He practically pushed you out the door. Why are you looking at his letters?"

"I was trying to figure them out," Jasmine said with a sigh. Her lies were not going to work on the girl at all, and it wouldn't be worth the effort to hide her actual situation any longer. "Do you know why Danny was writing to him?"

"My dad was writing to Danny, not the other way around," Diana said, coming into the room and looking over Jasmine's shoulder. "Those are just the responses."

"Why was your dad writing to Danny?" Is he the same Danny that just got engaged to Georgia?"

"Same guy. My dad is part of the reason that they got engaged."

"How?"

"Well, Danny is like crazy in love with Georgia—he has been for like forever, and he would have proposed a while back if my dad hadn't told him not to."

Jasmine looked down at the letters. "Why would your dad want to keep them from getting engaged?"

"Well, Georgia's pretty much for sure going to leave now. Danny's all about travel and freedom, and I think Georgia is too, despite all the ice sculpture stuff that she's into. My dad thought it would be best for the carnival if we didn't lose our best sculptor."

"What changed his mind?"

"He finally got sick of all the drama, I guess. I know they locked up Brandy, but most people around here think it was Georgia who killed Mark. I don't know if it's true, but it will probably become just as much of a rumor as the whole thing with her and Mark being together did."

"And it's easier to get rid of her," Jasmine mused, staring at the file. "Is that what this application from Rick is for? He wants to take her place?"

"No. He's going to take Mark's job, I think. No one's super happy about it, and I don't even think he knows it's going to happen, but he's really the only one who isn't involved in a bunch of other jobs. My dad likes to hire people already from the carnival to handle that job. It makes sure they're loyal in case something goes wrong."

"How do you know about all this?"

"I enjoy knowing things. I listen to his meetings when he has them, and sometimes he'll just talk about his plans in front of me. It's not like his office door is all that thick."

It didn't surprise Jasmine that Diana had a curious side. She guessed as much from the first time she had met the girl. What surprised her a little was Diana's willingness to share about her discreetly gained information. As she considered that, it reminded her why she had come to the cabin at all—to make sure Diana was okay. The girl was standing right in front of her now, and she hadn't even bothered to ask.

"I heard you weren't playing with Charlie and Eve much anymore. Is there a reason for that?"

"I spent basically all day with them just a few days ago. I don't know what they're complaining about."

A few days ago would have been before the murder, and Jasmine's fundamental theory about Diana's behavior revolved around it affecting her more than she let on. Her habits from before that time weren't relevant.

"Besides, we aren't six. We don't call it 'playing' anymore. We hang out."

"Right. Have you kind of stopped hanging out with them lately?"

"Not really," Diana said, and she looked like she was getting angry or uncomfortable with the line of questioning. "Why do you even care? I thought you were here to investigate that murder case, not my friendship drama."

"I'm worried about you," Jasmine said, and it took her a moment to realize Diana had assumed she was still investigating a solved murder. She wasn't wrong, but she was the only person who had clocked on so quickly. Jasmine wondered if it had something to do with Georgia being kicked out—maybe Diana believed that the ice sculptor was the real culprit. "You seem a bit off ever since the murder."

"You don't even know what I was like before that. You can't tell me what is off for me."

"You were drawing a dead body earlier. You aren't spending any time with your friends."

"I have to draw something, and everything around here is made of ice. I just wanted some variety,' Diana said, talking faster than she usually did. "And everyone gets into friendship drama. It rarely has something to do with a murder."

Jasmine wanted to believe Diana, but she was swirling her bracelet around her wrist in a way that seemed to convey her being nervous. It didn't seem like quite the right emotion for the situation, and Jasmine wondered why Diana would be. She thought back to a few minutes ago when Diana had been talking about how she listened in on her father's conversation, and it occurred to her for the first time Diana might know more than she was saying. Jasmine had assumed that seeing the body must have been the thing to throw her off, but it could only be more disorienting for her if she knew something about what had happened. If it involved her father.

"You haven't heard your father talk about the murder too much, have you? When you're listening in on him."

"No," Diana answered, but Jasmine didn't think her tone sounded all that convincing.

"What about anyone else? Have you heard anything?"

"No. I have heard nothing. The police already solved the case, remember?"

"I know. I wanted to know if you might have a new perspective."

"I don't want to talk about the murder anymore. It worried you I was thinking about it too much, so why don't you stop making me think about it even more?"

"Okay," Jasmine agreed, though she was even more certain now that Diana knew something. "You will come to me if you have anything to add to the investigation, right?"

"Right. But go before my dad gets back. He doesn't mind visitors, but he doesn't welcome snooping."

Jasmine got up from the desk and thanked Diana one more time before she left. Her feet had just hit solid ground when Diana spoke up again.

"You know, I don't know a lot about any of this, but talk to Henrietta. She might have something interesting to say."

"Got it," Jasmine said. She would have preferred for Diana to tell her whatever she knew, but she was willing to follow the breadcrumbs for her clues if that was the only way Diana would divulge her information.

Her first stop would have to be picking Luffy up. He would expect her back at some point soon, and she didn't want to disappoint.

She headed back in that direction, but stopped after getting back into the carnival. The door to the inside of the ramp was partially open. There wasn't a gap, but the edge of the door overhung the wall to reveal that the door was not latched. Jasmine thought about going over to close it. She knew Henrietta used the room just as much as Annette, and she needed to learn a little more about Henrietta before she talked to the woman. For all she knew, Henrietta was already inside the little break room. It wouldn't hurt to check out the little room here while she had a bit of time. She could meet up with Luffy in a second, and he wouldn't even be able to tell she had taken the slight detour.

Jasmine walked over to the door, carefully pressing her fingers against the bit that was sticking out, and pulled the door out of the wall. There was a chill from inside the room, and almost everything in there seemed at least partially made of ice. There were some skates along the back wall, and an old coffee machine was half full of coffee that was now mostly frozen. They also made the bench in the center out of an enormous block of ice, and it didn't look very comfortable. Jasmine walked over to it, and the door shut behind her as she went to look around.

She checked on the skates first. She was pretty sure that ice skates went in the trailer where they had found the body, so she wasn't sure why they would be in the little room instead. She leaned down and picked one up.

It looked like a normal skate, higher quality than those Jasmine had seen at local recreation centers. She turned it over in her hands and the blade shone nicely, and Jasmine wondered if it had been specially polished. As she set it down next to the other one, she noticed there was a bit of a smudge along the blade. She picked it up and pulled her sleeve over her hand to wipe it off, but she paused when she got to it. She had been expecting a fingerprint or small smudge from the skate being mishandled, but there was something else on the skate. It was tiny, almost dusty, and Jasmine ran a finger over the freezing metal. It felt almost like sawdust, and it reminded Jasmine of being in a workshop. At first, she could not think of any reason there would be wood caught on the edge of a skate.

Then, she remembered the gash on the edge of the wooden window frame. It had been fairly narrow for what it was, and Jasmine remembered wondering what could have caused it. The blade of an ice skate would be just the perfect thing to cause something like that. Maybe whoever had been trying to climb the trailer had hurt the wood when they kicked in the window. Or maybe someone had thrown the skate at the window or kicked it in on purpose. She couldn't imagine why, and she still wasn't sure how all the evidence outside connected to what had happened in the cabin.

Jasmine presumed the skate could have been exposed to wood somewhere else. She would have thought professional skaters would have gotten used to moving around in ice skates, at least to the point where they didn't risk damaging the blade by stepping onto wood with nothing to protect it. That left the question of how they had ended up in the break room. They had to belong to either Henrietta or Annette, and Jasmine leaned towards the former in that moment. She hadn't met the woman yet, which felt a little odd on its own. Sure, she could have made more of an effort on her end, but Jasmine was pretty sure she had seen most of the workers at the carnival at some point. The fact that she hadn't seen Henrietta yet seemed to suggest Henrietta didn't want to be seen.

Then there was Diana's comment. Jasmine didn't know what to take from it. It seemed very clear that she was at least tangentially related to the case, and Jasmine got the idea it was a lot more than a tangent. If Diana was sending her that way, and there were skates which might very well belong to her, it seemed natural to consider her as a potential suspect.

Jasmine was getting cold, and she noticed a small grate for the first time near the floor that seemed to push cold air in towards her. She looked around and realized it had to be there to keep the ramp completely frozen and structurally sound. The cold was probably even more important in here than it had been in Georgia's trailer.

Jasmine put the skate back down and walked over to the coffee machine. There was a small tower of mugs next to it, most of them dirty, and a little rack that held a variety of types of coffee. Everything from the brand to the flavor varied completely at random, and Jasmine thumbed through the packets to look for any significance. When she was nearly to the back, there was a gap that was bigger than the others. She figured it might have been a packet that had fallen over, and she almost instinctively reached for it to set it back up on its side.

To her surprise, rather than a small packet of coffee, her hand landed on some jewelry. It appeared to be a gemstone of sorts, and Jasmine picked it up to see what it was. When she looked at it, it was clear that it was a necklace, and it looked like a fairly expensive one. The pendant on the end was big enough to be costly, and Jasmine wondered why the necklace was hidden there. She didn't think anyone could have lost their necklace in such a specific place, nor could she imagine why someone would hide something valuable among coffee packs that may as well have been swiped from whatever hotel rooms they stayed at while they were on the road.

She thought about why Henrietta would even have a necklace like this to begin with, when she realized the necklace might not belong to Henrietta at all. She had only heard about one necklace since she had come to the carnival, and it had belonged to Georgia, only to be stolen from under her nose. It would make sense for that necklace to be hidden, and to be kept away from places where Georgia might go. As it was far back on the coffee rack and with the general expectation that they were adding new packets of coffee relatively often, it wouldn't be hard at all to keep the necklace hidden where it was without it ever getting found.

Jasmine wondered why someone would want to steal the necklace if they weren't going to sell it, and that led her to thinking about the primary effects of the action. The first was to anger Georgia, which could have been anyone's motivation, but the second was much more specific. It kept Rick from getting any further into ice sculpting than he already had been.

Jasmine realized as she held the necklace up to the light that there were really only two people who might have benefitted from Rick giving up his hobby—Peter and Annette. Peter would be keeping Georgia free of distractions so she could carry on with her sculptures. As for Annette, she had seemed enamored with her son being into skating, and his hobby might have impeded his athletic skill set.

Jasmine didn't know if Peter even had access to the room she was currently searching, and once she had decided what Annette's motivation might be, she looked suspicious for not just the theft of the necklace, but for the murder itself. Mark's job did not seem glamourous to Jasmine, but Annette seemed to think it would get a lot of attention, and had brushed away any safety concerns easily. She had even mentioned it didn't require a lot of skill from the actual skater, so she might have thought Rick could pull it off despite her low opinion of his skating skills.

Jasmine had reached for a lot of different motives, but this was the first one that really made sense. Cold-hearted as it was, the plan behind it seemed to play out just as Annette might have hoped, as Rick was being considered for the job. She had also made her suspicion of Georgia clear from the start, which had pointed Jasmine's investigation toward the very person who she could have borrowed equipment from.

It had to be Annette.

She rushed towards the door of the chamber to tell someone, but when she got there, she could not find a handle. Jasmine pressed against the door with both hands, but no matter how she struggled, she could not get it open. As she stepped back from the door and looked around her a bit, she realized two things— the first was just how awfully cold it seemed to get in the small chamber, and the second was how very much like her first vision the place she was trapped in looked. She stepped back from the door and felt her heart sink. If her vision was accurate, which it always was, she wouldn't be getting out anytime soon.

CHAPTER 8

Luffy didn't really understand why people would wait in line. He didn't like to wait for anything, and the entire process didn't look like any fun at all. At least when he had to wait for someone or for something, he was usually left alone to occupy himself with whatever he wanted.

Normally, occupying himself in such a way was simple. He could run around or think about some of his favorite things, like playing fetch or eating bacon. But today, the waiting seemed to take quite a bit longer than he was used to, and Luffy didn't like that. He knew Jasmine was going on the ice slide mostly to be polite to the man who had given her a free ticket, and partially because she needed to kill time, but she could not really have meant to take so long. He didn't have a watch, but his doggy intuition told him it felt like more than an hour had gone by.

Luffy did his best to wait patiently, like the obedient dog that he was, but when he saw someone get off the slide who was behind Jasmine in the queue earlier, he realized something was wrong.

If it had been anyone other than Rick working at the table, Luffy probably would have gone up to the person and made a fuss until they called Jasmine to come get him. He remembered Rick, though, and that he had not particularly liked him. The kid might not be as kind as the people who had made a point of helping him find Jasmine. In all probability, he would ignore him entirely or even try to get him thrown out of the carnival.

Instead, Luffy looked around for a familiar face. He had been around the carnival long enough to recognize most people, and he assumed he would come across someone he knew soon enough. When that didn't happen, Luffy wasn't quite sure what to do. He hesitated, walking over towards the line. He still didn't see Jasmine anywhere, and his curiosity led him backstage. Surely someone there would help him find Jasmine. They had done it before, and he didn't see any reason why they would not help him again.

The first people who Luffy found were Charlie and Eve. They were standing next to the trailer on the opposite side of the field from the one where Georgia did her carving, and they were dragging one of the big vats that held liquid nitrogen. It took their combined strength to get it to move at all, and they stopped while it was still about two feet from the trailer. Luffy wanted to watch to see what they were doing, but Jasmine was in danger, so he ran over to get them.

Charlie was just starting to climb onto the barrel, presumably to help her get onto the top of the trailer, when Luffy got there. She looked down at him.

"Look, Eve. Doesn't that dog belong to that girl from before?"

"The one with all the questions."

"We should give him back."

"How?"

"I think we should get Auntie Annette. She'll know what to do."

Charlie got down from her perch and they both tried to lure Luffy all the way to the trailer where the body had been found. As he was passing by the barrel, Luffy stopped. He found himself rather distracted by the large container which once had contained liquid nitrogen. The inside was mostly clean, but Luffy could make out a strange smell, and when he looked around the rim, he noticed a red residue which could only really be from one thing. It was too light to have been undiluted, but he realized at one point, the vat had held blood.

He couldn't dwell on it because as much as it explained the smell of blood under the trailer, he needed to keep moving so he could keep up with the children who were acting as his guide.

They took him to the trailer where the body once had been and straight to Annette.

"Auntie Annette," Charlie said. "We found that detective girl's dog."

"Oh... Well, I guess I can take it to her. Have you seen her?"

"No," Eve answered. "The dog just came up to us. I think he wanted to play."

"Were you still kicking the ball around? He probably wanted to play fetch."

"No--" Eve said, but her sister quickly interrupted.

"Yes. That's probably it."

"You girls weren't trying to climb on things again, were you? I've told you before that it's a dangerous game. You could hurt yourselves and then you won't be able to perform."

"We know. Can we take the dog back to its owner now?"

"Yes, we can. She was here not too long ago, but I think she left the dog over by the ice slides. Let's head over there."

Charlie and Eve skipped along as Annette led them back over to the ice slide. Jasmine was nowhere to be seen. Annette stopped for a moment near the back of the slides, but said nothing at all when she was asked if something was wrong.

They kept looking around the carnival and found nothing. Annette even took Luffy up to the front gate to make an announcement, but it did not seem to summon Jasmine. Wherever she was, she could either not hear what was being said, or she was unable to come back to Luffy. That concerned him even more.

"I don't know what to tell you kids," Annette said as the sun dipped low. It was still light outside, but it likely wouldn't be for much longer. People were trickling out of the carnival. "We'll have to leave the dog with Peter for a while and see if we can check in with Jasmine in the morning. You girls have schoolwork to do in the afternoons, and we can't really put that off any further."

Charlie and Eve groaned about having to leave, but they eventually did. Annette walked Luffy to Peter's trailer as she had promised, and when he wasn't there, she left Luffy and told him to stay where he was. Luffy figured she didn't think he would obey, which insulted him a little.

He intended to stay, but he saw Annette walking back into the carnival area, which confused him. They had already been there, and he didn't know why she would need to go back again. Maybe she was just going to fill out some duty she had as an employee, and it was easier to do on her own than attempting it with two young girls and a dog.

Luffy's gut instinct was to follow her, and he duly did. After following Jasmine around while she solved all of her cases, Luffy had gotten an eye for when things were out of place. Watching Annette retrace her steps struck him as something worth checking out. He left Peter's trailer and followed her at a distance, being careful not to be seen. He didn't want her or anyone else to take him back at such an inopportune moment.

Annette left the backstage area but did not go much further. She stopped at the back end of the ice slide. She reached into a bag at her side and pulled out a tool Luffy couldn't quite see. She did something to the wall of ice using the little tool, and the next thing Luffy saw was the wall of ice swinging outward and opening almost like a door.

He hid behind a pole to observe the events unfold.

"Jasmine," Annette said, and Luffy's ears perked up even further. He needed to know what was going on with Jasmine, to know that she was safe. He didn't know what was being hidden inside the carnival attraction, but he was already imagining many crazy things, like a dungeon or a cell. He couldn't tell if Annette was trying to save Jasmine or if she was the person who had locked Jasmine in there in the first place, so he held back from attacking until he learned more.

"I knew you would be in here as soon as I noticed the door was ajar. I wanted to have a little talk with you about what you might think you saw while you were in here."

Luffy needed no further proof. Annette had waited since they had first passed by the door to get Jasmine. It might not be exactly the same as locking Jasmine up, but it was definitely not what a good person would have done. He didn't know why Annette would do what she did, but he didn't need to. Jasmine would sort all of that out later. All Luffy needed to know was Annette was holding Jasmine against her will.

He bounded out from his hiding place and charged at Annette. He wasn't an attack dog, but Jasmine had been working with him on knocking people over by using his weight. He was getting pretty good at doing it without hurting anyone, and he was rather proud of that. He used all that practice to take down Annette and managed to push her all the way to the ground. He kept his paws on her to keep her from getting up and waited for Jasmine to come to his aid.

Except Jasmine never came. Was he too late? He hadn't ever heard Jasmine respond to the things that Annette was saying.

He looked back over his shoulder to see that the door had shut again. Luffy felt sure Jasmine was tied up in there, and he didn't know how long she would have while she was locked in there alone.

A much more immediate problem arose when Annette tried to push him off. She was strengthened by years of figure skating training, and when she was determined, there was really no problem getting him off. She got to her feet but Luffy was persistent and lunged at her again. In an attempt to ward him off, she lost her balance and stumbled back. Her ankle twisted and she went down, this time for good. She was silent in her pain, but Luffy could tell from the look on her face that the injury would be enough to stop her from getting away. Hopefully, it wasn't much more severe than that.

Luffy looked back at the shut door. He didn't have hands, and wouldn't be able to open even the easiest of doors. He needed help, probably for both Annette and Jasmine.

At a loss for options, Luffy barked and hoped for the best.

***

Jasmine had felt the same cold in her vision, but it was even worse now that she was really there. To keep the ice structure from melting, they had to keep things unbearably cold underneath it. Jasmine was pretty sure at this point that no one was intended to be down there, especially not for as long as she had been. She pulled her jacket tighter, but the fabric was already saturated with the cold and the movement made little difference.

The cold had slowed her down, both physically and mentally. When Annette had opened the door, it had confused Jasmine why she was not wearing Georgia's winter attire, as the person in her vision had been. Was it not the time in which she was going to get out of her glacial prison? Would she have to suffer for even longer than she already had?

Her mind slowed by the cold, Jasmine could not get through the thoughts quickly, and by the time she had made it to the end, it was already too late for her to make her escape. Annette had been interrupted by something, and while she handled that, the door had shut yet again. If Jasmine had processed things a little faster, she was sure she could have gotten out.

Now here she was, sitting in the same cold chamber and listening to echoes that sounded quite a lot like the bark of a dog. It made her wonder about Luffy, as she had encountered no other dog for the duration of the carnival.

Jasmine's sense of time had long since eroded almost entirely, and she was unsure of how long had passed before there was a sliver of light from the door. All at once it was too much, and she had to look away to keep it from burning her eyes. Unconsciously, Jasmine made an inhuman sound that she would neither be able to replicate or remember when she was out of the situation. When she dared to look back towards the door, she saw the dark figure from her vision. It had to be Annette, coming back to finish whatever she had come there to start. Jasmine cowered away, but her limbs were going numb and she could barely move.

"Calm down," said a voice that floated through the air, and the figure grabbed Jasmine off the bench. When Jasmine still seemed intent on struggling, they pulled away the gas mask to reveal Georgia's face. It wasn't Annette at all. "We're going to get you out of here and warm you up."

***

Blackwood Cove only had a single doctor, and Jasmine had been going there since she was a kid. After being locked in the chamber within the ice slide, she found herself taken there again. After some sleep, water and good centralized heating, she was looking quite a lot better, but that all took a couple of days to come about. On the Tuesday after everything had happened, she was staying at her parents' house, under strict doctor's orders to get as much rest as she could.

Brandon visited and brought with him the thing Jasmine had missed most while she was staying back at home—news.

"You're here," she said, greeting him with a hug. "Do you know anything new about the case?"

"Lustbader and a bunch of other people read your report,' Brandon answered, not even taking a moment to be insulted she had turned so quickly to matters of business rather than to pay attention to him. "They have a few questions about the scene you described with Luffy attacking her and how you would have been able to see that coming. But overall, they're absolutely convinced there shouldn't be any problem in getting Annette behind bars for good."

"And Brandy?"

"She's out of jail. She seems to be doing okay, considering. She's leaving the carnival for good, but I don't think that surprises anyone."

"What about Rick? Is he going to be okay with his mom in jail?"

"Once Georgia learned about how Annette had tricked her, she felt awful about not trusting Rick. I think she's taking him in. He'll have to follow her and Danny around wherever he goes, but he'll get to learn to sculpt and won't have to work carnival rides."

"Did anyone talk to Diana? Because Luffy and I have this theory that we've been putting together here now while I'm on bed rest. We think she might have seen Annette place the body. Luffy says the girls had been making a game out of trying to climb onto the trailers, and we think Diana might have been doing that when she saw Annette place the body. The evidence lines up, and she even wanted me to talk to Henrietta, the only one who would have been able to say how late Annette was to the skating show that day."

"Her dad has her talking to a therapist. He's taking the whole situation pretty well given all the news coverage. He can't find a good way to spin it, so he has turned to a moment of self-reflection to look for personal things he could improve on."

"Good for him. I hope the carnival doesn't end up shutting down. There are some good people working there."

"I think they're big enough to survive. I have some news about another business though."

"The Book Nook?"

"Nope. Your private eye business. Ever since people have heard about you getting locked in with all the ice, they think you're like, crazily dedicated to the job. Many people want your help. You've got your pick of cases."

"Let's do something warm next time," Luffy suggested, and Jasmine had to hold back a giggle.

"Thanks, Brandon."

"No problem," he said with a smile. "Just one more thing, though."

Jasmine's heart sunk as she expected some bad news. "What is it?"

"Next time, I think I'll sit out the actual case. I handle things better from the sidelines."

"Sounds perfect," Jasmine replied. Things had started to look promising.

END OF BOOK 6

BOOK 7: Eager to try her hand at an exciting televised game show, amateur sleuth Jasmine and her faithful companion Luffy are back at it again when they pit their skills against eleven fellow competitors on the hunt for a hidden treasure. But things soon take a darker turn when one of the competitors meets an untimely demise.

Six Paws Under is now on Amazon at

https://www.amazon.com/gp/product/B08Y7WSG7T

FREE NOVELLA: A roaring blizzard. A rest area in the middle of nowhere. Seven strangers stranded with a dead body. The killer is close by, and no one's going anywhere. In *Cold Case*, there are secrets lurking in the snow.

Join Max Parrott's author newsletter and get *Cold* Case for FREE only at https://dl.bookfunnel.com/boa2a0o66q

Dear Reader,

Hope you have enjoyed the ride. If you have...
...could you kindly leave a review?

Thanks,
Max

P.S. Reviews are like giving a warm hug to your favorite author.

We love hugs.

https://www.amazon.com/gp/product/B08NK1X2PM

Printed in Great Britain
by Amazon